Broken Pieces

Sandy Reyes

Contents

1.Queen

[Ishani's pov...]

Sadness is a strong emotion. it makes you do things which you don't want to do yet it feels so known.

i am in my private jet right now and i feel the exact emotion.

I am Ishani Rajwansh. The heiress to the throne of Rajasthan which is currently been taken care by my grandfather's sister, Chandani Chandramukhi.

Even though India is a democratic country and we are living in the 21st century, the people of Rajasthan still believe and follow the royals. My parents died when i was 18, my father was ruling Rajasthan this whole time but after his death the throne was passed down to me. my grandfather's sister means my Dadisa has been taking care of the throne for three years but two days ago i turned 21 and now i have to take up on my responsibilities.

my cousin that is my Dadisa's grandaughter, preksha or as i call her pari is coming to pick me up from the airport. i told her not to come as the media will be there.

The crown princess and the queen of rajasthan together is not a sight they would not like to capture.

as soon as the jet landed all of the bodyguards standing outside bowed down as a sign of respect and i made my way towards pari who was smiling at me but bowed down in respect " khamma ghani rani sa." she said and i chuckled but soon she straightened up and hugged me very tightly.

"kaisi hai ishuuu?" she asked me and i hugged her back. We were meeting after 6 months

"rani sa se aise baat karte hain?" a voice came and i saw Vikram, behind pari. he is my and pari's best friend.

i side hugged him as he helped me and pari get in the car escaping the sight of paparazzi.

we all settled inside with pari and i in the back seat as vikram was sitting in the front seat.

"bataiye, kaisa lag raha hai aapko waapas aakar, rani sa?" pari asked me raising her eyebrows.

"acha lag raha hai par darr bhi lag raha hai, and please tum dono rani sa rani sa karna band karo." i said and both of them chuckled. it feels good to be back.

"dadi ne jo kaha tha uske baare mein kuch socha?" pari asked and the smile wiped off from my face.

"mujhe nahi lagta main haan karungi..." i said and she looked at me with question.

"par agar tune haan nahi kiya toh power toh shitij ke paas chali jaaegi na?" vikram said and i realised that i have no other option.

"mere paas koi option bhi nahi hai and agar dadisa ne rishta mujhse bina puche karwa hi diya toh main kya hi kar sakti hoon?" i said with a huff.

"i don't think ki wo itne bure hain..." vikram said an i glared at him so he shut up.

"but ishu ek baar try toh karle..." pari began "end of discussion." i said and the car fell silent.

"toh be ready ishu, tere swagat ki full tayariyan hai." vikram said and opened the door as i walked out of the car only to be flashed by the cameras and the media asking stupid questions.

i walked inside my mansion, more like an ancient castle which is still well maintained .i saw dadisa and i sped my steps to reach her ignoring the media.

"mukhtar, media walon ko bahar karo aur kaho ki sabhi sawalon ke jawaab kal ki coronation ceremony par diye jaenge." i said to my body guard who was standing beside me and he nodded before walking away.

i saw dadisa with an aarti ki thaali in her hand and i gasped as she bowed down as i straightened her up again.

"ye kya kar rahi hain aap dadisa?" i asked her with a frown. i should be the one bowing down not her.

"ab rajasthan ki rani ke saamne toh jhukna hi padega na?" she said with a slight smile as i shook my head and bowed down touching her feet.

"jeeti raho." she said and patted my head lovingly and did my aarti.

after that i went inside to be greeted by the servants and the guards and my mouth was filled with sweets.

i went inside only to see my soon-to-be in laws standing with smiles and all of them bowed down as i entered.

"are aaplog kyon jhuk rahe hain..." i said as they straightened up.

"hum bhale hi ab ek parivaar ke hone wale hain par beta aap toh rani sa hi hain na?" kalyani ji said as i shook my head with a smile and touched all of their feets.

yes, i am getting married. There is a royal rule that every person who intends to sit on the throne has to get married or at least get engaged before the crowning. The person who is related to the royal family will have the higher hand in power. After my wedding my fiance's family will move in the palace as he will become the king of Rajasthan.

I am getting married to Ayaansh Yaduvanshi, my biggest enemy and the person i hate the most. His ego is as big as the Burj Khalifa or maybe even larger, he challenges my personality way too much.

If you are wondering why i am getting married to him then there are a lot of reasons.

First, He owns almost half of the jaipur so if i marry him then it is a profit for the state.second, Our grandfathers were the best of friends and we were promised to each other from the day we were born.third, i don't even want to admit it but even if i don't trust him as my husband, i do trust him to be the king of Rajasthan.

and the last reason because of which i am actually marrying him is because Dadisa emotionally blackmailed me by saying 'if you don't marry him then you will see my dead face.'

i was pulled out of my thoughts when vandana ji, his chachi said some-thing.

"sorry beta but ayaansh was not able to be here right now but he'll be here in an hour and i'll send him to your room... tab tak ke liye go and take rest." how do i tell them that i am greatful that he is not here.

i just responded with and 'it's okay' and smiled before pulling pari along with me and going in my room.

i closed the door of my room and threw myself on my bed.

"Ishu don't worry so much..." she said as i got a weird but amazing thought.

"pari what if i kill him after the marriage?" asked as she looked at me and shook her head.

"you need to have a kid before that or your marriage will be fixed to someone else and we all know that nobody would like shitij on the throne." she said and i sighed in disappointment.

shitij is our cousin with not so good intensions. He just wants to rule Rajasthan for his own benefit. he is a sick greedy bastard who only married his current wife to take over the throne. i feel bad for that woman and i feel shame to call him my brother.

a knock was on my door and i sat up straight while pari answered the door. i heard the voice and rolled my eyes.

"kaisi ho preksha?" he asked pari as she replied cheerfully. i don't blame her, he is nice to everyone except for me and that is why pari had no problem regarding the wedding. still, she supported me when Dadisa first brought up the proposal.

"ishu andar hai jiju aap ja kar mil lo i'll be downstairs." she said and walked off while he entered and closed the door as he leaned against the wall.

"hi Isha" he said and i gave him a fake smile.

"hi ansh" i said and he rolled his eyes.

"seems like i am winning." he said and i laughed.

"in your fucking dreams."

"how do you feel after calling me your fiance?" he asked with a similar fake smile.

"weird. I don't even know why i am being forced." i said and walked inside my wardrobe as he followed behind.

"right. you don't deserve anyone." he said as i could feel a pinch of hurt in my heart but i just smiled in response.

"don't think that you won ansh. We have a long way to go..." i said as i watched his expressions darken. i was looking in the mirror while removing my earrings as he stood right behind me, my back touching his chest. we were so close that i could hear his steady heartbeats.

"i will make your life living hell Isha" he said and i know that he will try to do that.

"i will love to see you try."

there was a knock on my door and both of us walked out of my wardrobe and i opened the door to see Kalyani ji there.

"aiye na Kalyani ji..." I said and she stepped inside.

"ab mujhe maa bulane ki aadat dal lo beta... and i just came here to give you these papers, ayaansh ke papa ne bhijwaye the he said he would love to meet you tomorrow before the coronation." she said and i nodded taking the papers from her hand.

"ji maa kal jab wo ghar aa jaenge tab main mil lungi..." i said .

" ye papers company coalition related hai tum dono padh lena and discuss kar lena..." she said as i smiled at her before she walked out.

"meet me at my office tomorrow, vikram will send you the timings... we'll discuss this partnership." i said as i gave the other half of the document to him.

"sure. by the way make space in 'our' closet because thodi der mein mera saaman yahaan shift ho jaega.." he said, purposely highlighting the word 'our' in the sentence as he walked out.

i took a deep breath trying not to run out of patience.

don't let him get into your head ishani.

but his words from earlier did bloom a weird insecurity in me.

you don't deserve anyone.

----

2. Coronation

chaos.

The whole palace is in utter chaos. tonight is mine and ayaansh's coronation ceremony.i still can't believe that i will officially be the queen of Rajasthan, but the thing which nullifies my excitement is that i will have him by my side. As the king of Rajasthan, as my husband.

i knock on the door of Akshay and Kalyani Yaduvanshi and soon the door opened showing maa who made me come inside with a smile.

i touched the feet of my soon to be father in law who blessed me with a smile.

"kaisi hain aap rani sa?" he asked me as i smiled.

"aap mujhe aapko papa bulane ko kehte hain aur mujhe rani sa bula rahe hain? mujhe Ishani hi kahiye papa..." i said as he smiled and reframed his sentence.

"kaisi ho Ishani?" he asked and i replied with the fakest smile possible because the next words were not true at all.

"thik hoon papa..."

"i am very happy that i am finally going to call you my daughter." and that mere sentence was capable of bringing tears in my eyes but i pushed them back.

Daughter. The word which gave me a sense of having a family.

"i hope today you and ayaan are going to finalize the partnership." he asked.

"yes we will. it will be done in a few hours."

"beta i know this is very different... the wedding and having a life partner but i trust you both to know that you will love and cherish each other forever." he said and i wanted to scoff and laugh at the joke of the century.

love. this is something we will never have in our relationship. i respect papa a lot but i hate him for giving me this hope that it might work out.

i just nodded at his statement and excused myself to go to office.

i went to my room and got in the shower almost immediately trying to wash out every hope and every emotion i was feeling at that time. i can't fall weak if i want him to lose.

i got changed in my work clothes and went downstairs to see every-one at the breakfast table.

"i don't have the time right now. bohot saara kaam hai i'll eat some-thing at the office so i need to go." i said and went outside as pari trailed behind.

My father started this company when he was 18 and turned it into a billion dollar venture within a few years. After dad's death i took over and now 'Rajwansh's' is India's biggest company partnering with 'Yaduvanshi's and co.'. I asked pari if she wanted to do something else but she denied and said she wanted to work in my shadow. She is the Managing Director of the company while Vikram is my Personal Assistant.

i was in my cabin when i heard a knock and Vikram came in with the schedule file.

"good morning Rani sa." he said with a smile as i greeted back..

"good morning vikram, what is the schedule for today?" i asked and he opened the file.

"not too much but you first have a meeting with Hukum sa, then you have a presentation with the roy's and that's it. afterwards is your coronation ceremony." he said and i nodded.

"ma'am Hukum Sa is here." pari came in the room as i nodded and she stood beside me with the file of the deal.

ayaansh came in and greeted me before sitting down while his Manager bowed down as i nodded at him.

"so, what are the conditions for the deal Mrs. Yaduvanshi?" ayaansh said specifically focusing on the word 'mrs. yaduvanshi'.

"The profit is about 50 percent more than our previous deals so the revenue should be doubled too... looking at the files and document sent by Mr. Akshay the conditions are specifically finalized already. I think that would be enough to clear from my side if anything else please fee free to ask." i said handing him the file as he took out a pen and signed on the papers and then asked his manager and pari to leave.

"i would like to have a conversation with you privately, if possible please ask the others to leave." he said and i told them to go out.

as soon as they went outside he smiled and put the file on the desk.

"you are way too smart Isha... you purposely made papa to sign the revenue double so that your company can have four times the more profit." he said chuckling.

"yet you signed on them..." i said as his smile dropped.

"because i trust my father" he said getting up and moving towards the window.

i walked towards him and stood beside him leaning on the window railing. i could feel the comforting weight of a dagger tied on my thigh which was covered by my pants.

"keep fooling yourself ansh, you may not admit it but we both know that you trust me." i said and he grabbed my wrist and jerked me towards him. we were so goddamn close that his breath fanned on my face.

"keep this pretty mouth of yours in check or one day you might end up in trouble Isha." he said tightening his grip on my wrist. i twisted my hand and got out of his hold pushing him aside and walking towards my desk and signing the remaining papers and handing it to them.

"i fucking hate you ayaansh." i said as he took the file and walked out not before kissing my jaw.

as soon as he left i tapped my foot three times and the dagger tied to my leg fell on the floor as i picked it up. i looked at the shiny metal and the feeling of safety it gave me was comforting.

will there ever be a moment in which i will not feel the need of having a dagger with me when i was around him? i don't think so.

he makes me feel lonely and empty. he makes me feel like i am his property. he makes me feel like nothing. And that fucking hurts.

it hurts so goddamn much yet i can't do anything about it because i can't give him the satisfaction of him making me sad.

i walked out of my cabin and to my home telling pari to handle roy's presentation as i headed home. i needed to chill before my engagement and coronation tonight.

---

i am sitting on a chair in front of my mirror as the makeup artist did her job. The only people present in the room were me, pari and the makeup artist. after a few minutes she was done and left after congratulating me.

i am wearing a purple lehenga with jewelry and light makeup. A knock was heard on my door and pari opened it. maa stepped inside with vihaan, ayaansh's brother and smiled looking at me. Maa took out kajal from her eyes and rubbed it behind my ear.

"ekdum pari jaisi lag rahi hai meri bahu..." she said and i smiled.

"kya aap bhi pari-pari kar rahe ho, bhabhi ne toh aishwarya rai fail kardi!" he said and i chuckled.

Vihaan was always a funny and jolly guy, with all of us at least. Him and Pari knew each other from way before but they stopped talking at some time. She never told me what happened and i believe that it was bad. Now there is only tension between them. For example: as soon as he entered the room, Pari left.

"Aishwarya Rai? seriously?" i asked with a sarcastic smile as he nodded.

"accha anyway, main toh yahaan iske liye aai thi..." she said taking out a box from her hand bag.

she opened it and i saw the most beautiful Diamond necklace inside it.

"ye meri saasu maa ne mujhe meri engagement pe dia tha... ab main tumhe de rahi hoon." she said and made me wear the necklace.

wearing it didn't seen weird, it made me feel complete. it made me feel beautiful.

"thank you maa..." i said as she frowned and hit my head lightly.

"maa bol rahi hai aur thank you bhi?" she asked in fake anger as i couldn't control my laugh anymore and they walked out.

i could visibly see Vihaan and pari tense and glare at each other before they walked out.

"you have to be down there in 15 minutes tab tak ke liye relax!" she said and sat on the bed.

"what's going on between you and vihaan?" i asked out of curiosity.

"can we not talk about it ?" she asked and i sighed before looking in the mirror once again.

"i look pretty so my photos will also be nice..." i said with a fake smile.

[ayaansh's pov...]

it is so freaking dumb.

as much as i love the idea of winning and making her cry, the more i hate the idea of getting married to her.

I hate that woman's guts and how she manages to rile me up in a few sentences. i hate that she knows almost everything and how she is never fucking wrong.

i fucking hate her.

"ohooo... bhai bhabhi ke khayalo mein khoye hue lag rahe hain..." i heard the annoying voice of my brother, Vihaan. what an idiot.

"if planning a murder is considered as 'khayalon mein khona' toh haan..." i said as he rolled his eyes.

"abhi main badi maa ke saath gaya tha unke room mein...she wanted to give her a necklace and trust me bhai you are very lucky, she looked beautiful." he said as if she was his wife.

"i thought tu uski behen ko dekhne mein-" i was about to complete when he cut me off "don't" and that was the end of our conversation.

"chalo bhai let's make you the King..." he said as we moved downstairs where all of the important business clients, politicians, relatives and some of the media were there.

i waited for about 2 minutes and then she came with her big attitude and ego.

i tried to look away but i couldn't.

one more thing which i hated was that she was beautiful.

i can argue against anything but not the fact that she was an ethereal beauty. i finally looked away and the cameras flashed on our faces.

pari came with a tray and we took the rings from it.

"don't fall in love with me." we both whispered to each other at the same time.

"trust me, i won't." i said as she chuckled.

"i won't be surprised if you do." she said and this was one example of her pissing me off.

i slipped the ring on her finger as she did the same to me. for others it might be the beginning of a life full of love but for us it was the beginning of a life full of hate. i will win isha. "i will become a great king for Rajasthan but trust me you will not like me as your husband at all." i said and she smiled, a smile that didn't reach her eyes.

"i was waiting for you to say that." she said with a sigh as we turned towards the crowd with smiles plastered on our faces, pretending as if we are totally in love.

Chandani Dadisa came and gave both of us two boxes.

she then turned towards the crowd and everyone went silent.

"teen saal pehle humare priya raja sa aur rani sa chal base. sab soona sa lagne laga." she began and i could feel isha tense beside me." our king was a powerful but a kind man while our queen was the epitome of beauty with brains..." that was true. her parents were literal gems. is she adopted by any chance?

"now, i would like to announce the new rulers of Rajasthan. welcome our King Ayaansh yaduvanshi and our Queen Ishani Ayaansh Yaduvanshi." Dadisa completed and i saw isha smiling at the crowd but her fists were clenched. i smirked at the thought, she didn't like my name attached with hers.

I leaned towards her a little so only she could hear me and whispered in her ear " abhi toh sirf sagai hui hai toh tumhe itna gussa aa raha hai, bas ek hafte mein shaadi hai toh you can guess how much trouble you'll be in..." i said as she turned to me with a glare. it was way too fun to piss her off. "mrs. ishani ayaansh yaduvanshi" i completed only to see her turn away from me to gather all her patience.

"Bas naam se hi hoon toh please don't extend your hopes." she said and a smile bloomed on my face as i looked back at the crowd.

after answering a few of the media's questions and after everyone went home. the whole family got settled in their rooms.

i was twisting and turning on my bed, sleep ws nowhere near me so i just simply got up and went to the kitchen downstairs.

i need a drink.

----

ye lo itna bada update de diya maine 🖤

3. Hold on

[ayaansh's pov...]

The corridor was dark and empty.

I walked inside the kitchen and i saw that Isha was there pouring herself a glass of whiskey. She rolled her eyes after looking at me.

i just went up to her and pulled the whiskey bottle out of her hand as she sat on the kitchen counter and i stood beside her, leaning on the counter.

there was just silence, complete silence. Both of us were just in our own worlds drinking whiskey and not looking at each other at all until she broke the silence.

"is it because of what happened 5 years ago?" she said drinking her whiskey while i just tried to process her words.

"what?"

"do you hate me so much because of that?" she asked, now i get why she was drinking at 2 in the night.

"does it matter?" i asked and she looked at me. I never actually realized how pretty her eyes actually were.

what the fuck are you thinking ayaansh? maybe it's just the alcohol working.

"yes it does."

"then yes. it is because of that." i said and i could see her expressions change.

"even after i told you i never had a choice?" she asked and turned her face away, i could see the tears pooling in her eyes from the side. my grip on the glass tightened.

"it's not that. it's just the fact that i can't trust you anymore after that." i said and she got off the counter placing the glass there and walking back towards her room.

she made a mistake and she knows she is paying for that. She might think i am being way too torturous for just one mistake but only i know what it felt like when she hid an information like that from me.

i still remember that night clearly and it is still one of the worst things i have ever fucking experienced.

[Ishani's pov...]

I woke up after a few hours. Last night was a complete disaster, i almost cried in front of him.

i know i made a mistake but i never had a choice. If he was in my position then he would've done the same thing. but he isn't. I did try explaining everything to him multiple times and now after 5 fucking years i am out of words to explain it to him.

i made a mistake but the price he is making me pay is cruel. it is like fucking torture.

earlier when i used to talk to him i used to feel happy and comfortable. now, whenever i am around him this weird coldness spreads inside my veins. this emptiness seeps in my heart and i know that maybe i do deserve it. maybe he was right when he said that i deserved this hate from him.

I got inside the gym and every punch on the punching bag felt like i am reducing the pain in my heart. Every punch felt like i am removing every memory of him and I in which we were actually happy. Every punch felt like a punch in my gut as i forced myself not to cry. Not to cry over the fact that i didn't deserve love, that i didn't deserve anyone.

no. no ishani you can't let him win. my inner conscience said and i listened to it.

maybe i just needed to hold on for sometime.

Hold on. that's what i am doing since the day that i was born, holding on to people so that they don't leave me to be alone.

hold on.

And with the last punch the bag broke and scattered on the ground, and just like that every emotion which i was feeling was also scattered. I just stood there in silence and then i felt footsteps approaching.

"what did the poor punching bag do to you?" he asked and there it was again, the feeling of emptiness and loneliness.

"what do you want?" i asked him with complete disinterest.

"let's have a one on one." he said passing me a dagger and i caught it just in time before it could slice my head off.

"okay." even i didn't know why i was giving one word answers only.

maybe i was just tired of the workout i did before.

no it is because you are tired of yourself. my inner conscience mocked me.

i positioned my knife in my hand as he lunged forward. i ducked down kicking his leg causing him to stumble a little. touché.

he grabbed my leg making me flip and my head hitting the exercise mattress under me. fuck i think i'll get a headache later.

"asshole." i whispered under my breath.

i kicked his ankle from beneath me as he fell down and i got on top of him putting the dagger at his neck.

"do you give up?" i asked knowing the answer would be 'no.'

"no." he said as he switched up the places making him get on top of me as he pinned my hands above my head, keeping the dagger just under my chin.

i kicked him in the stomach now getting up and punching him on the face and i felt a pain in my thigh.

i looked down to see a cut on it.

this bastard left a fucking scar.

"looks like i win." he said with a smirk. i want to peel that smirk off his face.

"looks like you didn't" i said and i knew he felt the pain.

he looked at his forearm which had a cut .

"i am not going to let you win this easily, right?" i asked him in a serious expression as he dropped the dagger coming closer to me.

"you know that the cut you have is way deeper than mine" he said grazing his finger over my cut. it hurt but am i going to show it? nope.

"that means this will leave a scar darker than mine." he said pulling his hand up, caressing my face.

"just like the wound you gave on my heart was way deeper than yours." he said and i pushed him away, going back towards my room.

"tit for tat baby." i heard him yell as i was just at the gym door.

i went in my room and got out the first aid box. i can't let anyone see this cut or else i have to explain what happened.

i took out the antiseptic and put it on a cotton piece dabbing it over my wound.

tears flew out freely as i sobbed. the fact was that it was not because of the pain of my wound but it was because of this pain in my heart.

it fucking hurt so much.

so much that i sometimes wanted to lock myself away from the world.

it still hurts and i knew what he wanted to tell me by giving me the cut.

some wounds never heal and even if they do they leave the worst scar.

I knew that I only had one option.

Hold on.

4. Frustration

----

i bandaged the wound and changed my clothes.

i don't even know what to feel anymore. If i wanted i could've broken off this wedding but i know i can't. it's not like the law is applicable to me, it's the emotional drama Dadisa has done in front of me.

what am i going to tell her? that i don't love my so-called fiance at all and i am just doing it for the sake of the throne.

this is fucking annoying.

i got ready and was about to go downstairs when i heard a knock on my door.

"come in." i said and a maid came in.

"rani sa, shitij bhai sa aa chuke hain... badi maa sa ne kaha hai ki aap Hukum sa ke saath neeche aa jaiye." oh fuck. fuckity fucking fuck.

as soon as the maid went out i took a deep breath preparing myself.

i know that Shitij will create a scene. i fucking know it.

okay ishani don't think much about it, take ayaansh with you and go downstairs, simple.

no it's not fucking simple.

i can do this.

i got out of my room and knocked at ayaansh's door.

i heard a faint 'come in.' and i went inside and he looked at me as if he didn't expect me to be there.

even i didn't expect myself to be there.

"why do you look tense?" he asked and i reminded myself that i can go and face shitij.

"isha!" he yelled my name and i got out of my trance."where are you lost?"

"we have a crisis. Shitij aa gaya hai and he wants to meet us." i said and i could see his expressions change from confusion to disgust to 'fuck no!'

"is it necessary for us to be downstairs..." he asked me. I knew he hated Shitij as much as I did. everyone hates him.

"Dadisa ne bulaya hai." i said and he almost whined.

"chalo." he said opening the door as i went outside and took a deep breath.

"we can do this." he said motivating both of us.

The only time we both unite is when we have to face that son of a bitch. he is no less than trouble.

we went downstairs to see everyone with a bored expression but Shitij was standing there with the widest smile possible.

i walked up at him and looked at him with a stern expression as he engulfed me in a hug. i didn't even hug him back but then walked up to bhabhi and hugged her as she hugged me back. She looked so drained out, that bastard married her only for his use yet when i asked her if she wants me to do something about it she denied.

i knew Shitij was pissed at my behavior. what was he expecting? for me to do his aarti as he comes in? not happening.

"sorry main sagai pe nahi aa paya... i really wanted to but thoda kaam aa gaya tha..." he said as if i wanted him to come to my engagement.

"what do you want shitij?" ansh asked him and he looked at him as if he asked for his kidney.

"i just wanted to spend a day with my sister, is it too much to ask for!" he said accusingly.

"for you? yes. it is too much to ask for and agar yahaan iss hi bakwas ke liye aaye ho toh sorry we have a lot of work to do." i said and started going upstairs again when his voice called back.

"fine. can we talk in private."

"everyone go back to your room for sometime." i said and everyone moved back.

now it was just me, Ansh, Shitij and bhabhi.

"now can we talk about the important work here?" ansh asked him and he took a deep breath taking out a bundle of papers from his bag.

"i want you to give me the full rule of Mewad." he said and i couldn't suppress my laugh. I looked at ansh who was trying to not laugh but eventually it broke out.

"wait, wait, wait... you really don't expect us to do that right?" i asked after calming down a little.

"i am your brother, you should at least trust me this much." he said so casually and we again started laughing which must've pissed him off.

"I AM FUCKING SERIOUS ISHANI!" he said yelling and that's when i lost my temper.

"don't you dare raise your voice at me again." i said calmly but in a stern voice which he took and lowered down his voice immediately.

"and for your information i have only set up different rulers for the cities for efficient functioning. yes, they have power but not more than me so if you are thinking that i will give you the full control then you are wrong." i said and turned back but a strong grip on my arm turned me around me. it was so harsh that it can cause a bruise later.

before i could react a punch landed on his face causing him to leave my arm. now Shitij was on the floor with a definitely broken nose.

"if you touch her again i will personally put a bullet through your skull." ayaansh said and i pulled him back by his hand.

i saw shitij, his nose was bleeding. i noticed that every guard had their guns pointed at shitij. i motioned for them to put it down.

"if you are trying to be violent here and think that my decision will change then go fuck yourself." i said and he got up putting a hand over his nose.

"agar shaadi ke liye yahaan rukne ka plan hai toh ask a servant they'll show you the room." i said and practically dragged ayaansh upstairs.

i opened his room's door and he closed it behind us and i glared at him as he looked at me expecting to say something.

"now don't tell me you are going to argue with me for defending you..." he said in a nonchalant tone.

"no, no i am happy that you defended me." i said and he looked confused.

"but why?" i asked and he closed his eyes rubbing his temples as if he was frustrated.

"what do you mean isha?" he said and god i wanted to smash his head in the wall.

"are you bipolar or something? first you act like you don't fucking care and then you go around blackmailing people!" i yelled at him and he pushed me against the wall tightening his hold.

he was so close that our noses touched. it's getting hard to breath and it's frustrating as of how my heartbeats picked up pace.

"yes. i don't fucking care about what you do but i am not going to tolerate if someone tries to hurt you." he said and i try to get out of his grasp "if he tries to do that again then i will skin him alive and make you watch it Isha." he said and all i wanted to do was to get out of there and jump off a freaking bridge.

i stomped my foot over his and his hold losened due to the impact. i pushed him away from me and opened the door of his room "i don't understand you ayaansh and it's bloody frustrating" i said before slamming the door shut and walking towards my room. i wish i could just murder him.

i locked the door of my room and he knocked, again and again. "open the fucking door isha, we have to talk some day." he said and i needed to calm down before i killed someone.

"no. we can just forget about this just like each one of our conversations." i said and he punched the door and i could hear him walk away.

I sat on my bed and his words replayed in my mind.

i will not tolerate if someone hurts you.

a laugh escaped my mouth. as if he isn't hurting me at all.

the audacity of this guy to say something like that after constantly hurting me is just wow.

i heard another knock and fucking hell this man is crazy.

"kya hai ayaansh- oh hi bhabhi..." i was yelling but my voice lowered when i saw bhabhi who smiled after seeing me yell.

fuck ishani why the hell are you so fucking embarrassing?

she came inside and i closed the door behind me, turned around hugging her.

"kaisi ho meri pyaari bhabhi?" i asked and she hugged me back.

"main thik hoon ishu... tu kaisi hai?" she asked me and i nodded before puling back and sat on the bed.

"ladai ho gayi?" she asked me and i looked away. if i look at her in the eyes i will tell her everything and that is the last thing i wanted to do.

"i am extremely sorry ishu, I know what shitij did is not right and i am just-"

"aap kyon sorry bol rahe ho? sorry toh use bolna chahiye na?" i said and she patted my cheek lovingly. she was my best friend, my comfort person.

"bhabhi aap use chhod kyon nah dete. you just have to say that you want to leave him and i'll take care of the rest. i just want you to use your words and he'll be gone from your life." i said but she shook her head negatively.

"kyon?" i am done with that guy and i don't want her to suffer.

"time aane par main tujhe sab bata dungi..." she said and got up "Tu ayaansh se apni ladai solve kar i'll leave."

---

too much angst today....

5. Gift?

[ayaansh's pov...]

"Ishu! jaldi!!" bhabhi yelled knocking at her door. why am i being forced to go to their shopping spree?

turns out that they wanted to do some random shopping from the local market and wanted to eat gol gappe... basically i am just being dragged for no reason.

"sorry i was late." she said coming out ,fixing her earrings. she looked at me and her smile dropped.

still thinking about yesterday.

the three of us just went downstairs and were just at the main gate when shitij's annoying voice interrupted us.

"kahaan jaa rahi ho kusha?" he asked bhabhi and ishani just turned around with a smile. her smiling at shitij? it's going to be fun.

"mere saath market jaa rahi hain." she said still smiling.

"no she's not going anywhere." he said it like an order.

"really? who are you to stop her?" she said in a sarcastic tone.

"i am her husband. you cannot stop me." he said in a stern voice. was he trying to be powerful?

"and i am the queen of Rajasthan. you cannot change my decisions." she said and we turned around and bhabhi got inside the car.

"tum apni power ka guroor mere saamne mat dikhao." he said and now i am fucking annoyed. why the hell can't he just let us do our own thing?

Isha just turned around walking towards him. he clearly looked scared yet he tried to mask it with a fake stern expression.

"agar main apni power ka guroor na dikhau toh bhi power toh power hi rahegi. agar agli baar zyada zaban chalane ki koshish ki ya fir bhabhi ko control karne ki koshish ki toh i'll make sure that you'll not be able to speak for the rest of your life." she said in a calm but dead serious tone.

i don't know why but i was proud of her.

we got inside the car and bhabhi was clearly scared.

"bhabhi aapko darne ki zaroorat nahi hai... he'll not do anything." isha said holding her hand.

"haan bhabhi aap tension mat lo... he's an idiot." i said as she faked a smile.

"you know what let's fix your mood...aaj dresses bhi kharid lenge 2-3." ishani said.

no. no i don't want to be a part of this stupidity.

"no." "yes."

both me and bhabhi said at the same time.

"yes ansh... we are going to shopping so we have to buy something right? ab sirf gol gappe kha kar toh nahi aa sakte." isha said and i wanted to smash my head on the window.

"mujhe kyon fasa liya yaar?" i said, almost whined. another thing which i hate the most is shopping.

"maza aata hai tumhe pareshan karne mein..." isha said and both her and bhabhi laughed.

"very funny."i said and soon we were at the market.

"make sure there is no paparazzi and tighten the security around the market." i said to the security head inside the car before getting out.

"i mean we could've just went to a designer store or maybe bring the designers at home... why do you both have to be here?" i asked and bhabhi just rolled her eyes.

"jitna maza market mein se shopping karne mein aata hai utna kisi designer studio mein nahi aata." bhabhi said and both of them just went to random shops.

isha looked happy. even if i don't care but it kind of felt nice to see her happy.

i saw her eyeing a particular pair of earrings at a stall but before she could even go there bhabhi pulled her to another shop.

i don't know what got into me but i bought those jhumkas. oh fuck. why did i even buy them? what am i even going to say?

i just went towards them who were in a kurti shop. bhabhi was just looking at the kurti's and trying to find the perfect piece.

i couldn't find out any excuse so i just very carefully passed her the paper bag of the jhumka.

but guess what? she noticed and surprise was evident in her expression but instead of a snarky, sassy reply, she just smiled. is this actually Isha?

"i-uh... thank you." she said and smiled again but now looking away. this is definitely not Isha.

"this is not a gift." i whispered and i swear i saw that smile falter a bit.

"i don't expect you to give me a gift ansh." she said and i let out a sigh of relief. looks like the real Isha is back.

"ishu ye wala le le it will look pretty on you." bhabhi said and again they were busy checking out clothes.

the difference was that i couldn't keep my eyes off her.

she looked beautiful in that simple anarkali suit and the light bangles that adorned her hands. the kajal defined her eyes and even without any makeup her face glowed in the sun.

no. ayaansh you hate her and it is definitely not appropriate to check her out in a public place. one part of my mind spoke.

but she is your wife. you have all the rights to check her out, whether in public or in private. the other part spoke.

but you hate her so look the fuck away. and the first part won so i looked away, focusing everywhere but her.

soon they were done and were about to walk out of the shop, more like run out of the shop so i held Isha's hand to slow her down.

why did i feel an electric current throughout my body?

but this woman did not even realize that her fingers were interwind with mine.

"Isha stop running like a kid you are going to get hurt...." i said and she slowed down a bit still not realizing that she was holding my hand. she was not even holding it, our hands were basically tangled with each other and she was literally dragging me along with her.

i just held her hand so she doesn't get lost. i convinced my mind.

but now even when we are at a still position, due to some weird goddamn reason i don't want to leave her hand.

i looked at her hand and the ring on it. our engagement ring-my ring- on her hand. it looked beautiful but both of us know that it will never mean anything.

----

we soon got home all tired. god, it was so irritating.

"bohot maza aaya ishu." bhabhi said laying down on the sofa.

"bilkul nahi." i said getting up.

"oh hello rukiye ayaansh bhaisahab... apni priya patni ke samaan ko unke room tak pohonchaiye." bhabhi said and i rolled my eyes.

"ask a servant they'll do it." i said but a whack on my head was all i got.

"are theek hai yaar jaa raha hoon maar kyon rahe ho... thodi toh izzat kar lia karo." i said picking up the bag and going along with krutika.

the silence was way too loud on our way upstairs and she broke it again.

"if you were expecting me to give you a rude reply then you are wrong. i am not that mean." she said with a smile and i looked at her.

we were at her door and she took the bags from me.

"even if it was not a gift, it meant something to me. so, thank you." she said and closed her door and i stood there for a minute trying to process her words before walking away.

sometimes i don't understand her at all.

[Ishani's pov...]

i was in my room putting the new clothes on their place when my door opened and pari came in.

"kabhi toh knock kar liya kar chudail." i said and she just jumped on my bed.

"i missed you today. tu hoti toh aur bhi maza aata." i said and she just kissed me on my cheek.

"ab tu gayi thi toh kisi ko toh office sambhalna tha na?" she said and started helping me clean up.

"ooohhh... this is pretty." she said and i looked over to see the earrings in her hands.

i snatched it from her and she frowned "we always share things, ispe itna kya possessive ho rahi hai?"

how should i tell her that that this was the first unofficial non-gift gift that he gave me?

"let me guess...." she said and pretended to think "jiju ne gift diya na." she said in a teasing tone.

"It's not a gift." i said casually putting away the earrings in my wardrobe but i knew that my cheeks were getting pink.

"haan, haan ye toh shaanti ka prastaav hai na?" pari said sarcastically and i rolled my eyes.

why am i getting possessive over a pair of earrings?

i hate him. i tried to convince my mind and then looked at my engagement ring.

it's beautiful but i know it will never mean anything.

----

ye ayaansh pehle sweet banta hai fir 'i hate you' bol deta hai

feel free to give gaali

6. Hugs

[Ishani's pov...]

Royal court is one of the most stressful places.

right now me and ayaansh were standing in front of at least fifteen people who are begging for aid.

the thing which breaks my heart is that all of them were girls of ages between 5-15 years.

i asked the doctors to treat their wounds properly and turned to the servants "inke liye saaf kapde aur khana le aiye. Dhyaan rakhiega ki inhe koi bhi pareshani nahi honi chahiye."

The police officer approached us and bowed down.

"Kya hum akele mein baat kar sakte hain Rani sa, Hukum sa." he said and i nodded as ayaansh led him the way to an interrogation room at a silent area of the mansion.

"inke saath kya hua tha officer?" ayaansh asked. he was as worried as i was.

"ye bacchiyan hume ek abandoned building mein mili thi. kai toh kuch bol bhi nahi paa rahi except for the older ones. We found one guy with them who tried to run away when we caught him and sabse badi bacchi ne jo confessions diye hain they are just..." the officer spoke and trailed off at the end and i almost had an idea about what happened.

"kya bataya usne officer?" i asked him and he looked down.

"they were trapped there for almost 8 months now. All of them were raped...not once but many times. every single one of them. their were a lot of men but only the one we caught was left behind. they were planning to sell these girls and they were doing it for a huge amount." he said and my heartbeats almost stopped.

they were raped and one of them was 5 years old.

"one more thing..." the officer spoke up after hesitation and i looked up at him "one of them was 16 years old. One of the men got her pregnant and killed her." he said and tears sprang up in my eyes.

"thank you officer for getting them out of there, continue the search but leave that guy to us." ayaansh said and the officer left after nodding.

"Isha..." he said and i couldn't stop the tear that escaped my eye.

"how can someone be so horrible ansh?" i said and he wiped the tear off my face.

"this is the terrible reality... and no matter how much we try this still happens." he said with disappointment and disgust evident in his voice.

"they were there for 8 months. they were in that hell for such a long time and mujhe pata tak nahi tha... one of them 5 years old and they killed a 16 year old, she was pregnant- this is just-" i said fumbling with my words. i rarely panic but this was one of the moments where i was losing my mind.

my breathing was faltering and he took me in his arms. I hugged him as he rubbed my back to relax me.

"it was not your fault Isha... stop blaming yourself for everything that is not even your fault." he said and i stood in his embrace for a few minutes.

it felt comforting, i felt as if someone was there to hold me. for the first time in years, i felt like he will not leave me to be alone.

i pulled back and that's when i realized that how close we actually were, so much that if i moved an inch then my lips would touch his. i carefully pulled back and he wiped the tears off and caressed my face.

"we need to have a 'talk' with that guy..." i said and he understood what i meant by 'talk' so he smiled.

"fine. come on let's go have a 'talk' with that bastard." he said and gently lead me out of the room.

[ayaansh's pov...]

there he was. trying to get out of the handcuffs that were keeping him tied to the chair. he was badly beaten still he didn't give us any information.

"it's better if you kill me now... i won't say anything." he said panting.

fucking bastard.

"They will assassinate you." he said with a smile looking towards Isha.

"oh really? then i hope they do it nicely. i always had a dream of dying in an adventurous way." she said dreamily and then cut off one of his fingers using a dagger.

his screams and cries filled the room. This is still not enough for the pain they've given to those kids.

"who do you work for?" she asked and he cried.

"i don't know who is behind all this. i was just being paid by one of the higher people." he said and i looked at isha who had his blood on her hands.

"what is his name?" i asked and his voice was shaky when he replied "omkar shrivastav"

"anything else? hume sab bata do we know everything about you and your family..." isha said and he looked at her in disbelief.

"you won't do anything..." he said and i smiled "trust me dude you would not like to know how low we can actually go..."

"mujhe sach mein kuch nahi pata main toh bas wahi kar raha tha jo mujhe bola tha." he said crying.

"aur tumhe unn baccho ke liye ek baar bhi bura nahi laga?" Isha said and looked at me signaling to end it.

"bye bye motherfucker." i shot him in between his eyes and went towards the washbasin where isha was washing her hands.

"Vihaan will find the info on that guy." i said standing behind her and she hummed while drying her hands with a towel

"Isha are you okay?" i asked and she turned towards me.

that's when i realized how close we were actually standing. but did i want to move away? for a weird reason, no.

"I will be." she said, it was more of a whisper.

"why are you acting like this?" she asked and i frowned "act like what?"

"act like you care if i am okay or not?" she said and for some odd reason that question pricked my heart.

"i do care if you are okay or not. i am not going to let anything or anyone else make you cry, it's my thing to do." i said the truth, i knew it hurt her but she smiled at me and nodded.

one moment i was looking in her eyes and the dimple she had on her right cheek and the the other moment i had my arms wrapped around her.

hugging her did not feel weird at all. it felt comforting and peaceful. And for the first time in years, i didn't want to leave her alone.

----

short chapter....sorry

7. Blush

"Omkar Srivastav, 34 years old, Mewad resident, Married to kalpurna Srivastav who died 2 years ago." Vihaan said looking at his laptop screen.

"Koi purana transaction, address anything?" Ansh asked him while vihaan just looked way too focused on his laptop.

"I found something..." he said. he look hesitant "bhabhi this guy was your Father's Minister but was fired due to unknown reasons."

Wait What the fuck?

"What the fuck?" i mumbled and got seated next to him as he passed me his laptop.

it was true. he was papa's minister.

"He was fired right before your parent's death.i didn't find any other info rmation..." he said and i sighed.

"but i guess library mein kuch ho sakta hai... i mean wahan par almost har staff ka data hota hai. agar digitally kuch nahi mila toh shayad physical copy mil jaye." pari said.

"perfect, then we'll look there today" ansh said and i nodded.

suddenly the door opened and maa peaked in with a smile.

"tum chaaro ko koi special invitation dena padega kya? aajao breakfast ke liye..." she said before slamming the door shut.

"why is she so sarcastic all the time?" pari said and i shook my head.

we went to the breakfast table after deciding that me and ayaansh will go to the library today afternoon.

"are wahh aap logon ne neeche aane ka kasht kar liya?" maa again said sarcastically and i got seated.

"acha by the way 2 din mein haldi hai tumhari everything is ready right?" dadisa asked and i mentally face palmed myself.

"i kinda forgot that we were getting married in 5 days..." i mumbled to ayaansh who looked at me with a 'are you serious' expression.

"umm- haan sab ready hogaya Dadisa." i said and she nodded with a smile and gave us plates.

"i am so happy that you two are getting married!!!" papa said almost jumping in his seat.

"even i can't believe we both are getting married..." ayaansh mumbled and i bit my lip to control my laugh.

"acha ab shaadi ho jaye fir thode mahino mein hume khush khabri bhi suna dena..." maa said and i choked on my food.

"What?" i asked after drinking water.

"haan, ab hume bhi toh apne pote ya poti ki shakal dekhni hai na." papa said and i almost choked on my food again.

i looked at ayaansh who was trying so hard not to laugh but was failing miserably.

"b-bacche?" i asked almost stuttering.

"haan obviously." vandana chachi said and i was almost as pale as snow now.

"mahine?" i asked and all of them nodded enthusiastically.

i was not planning to have kids for like 5-6 years!

i looked back at ayaansh who was still trying not to laugh.

i kicked him on his foot with my heel and he stopped laughing.

"what's so funny ayaansh?" i asked him mumbling.

"it is funny i mean, you should just look at your expressions." he said with a smile.

"it's funny for you but it's not funny for me..." i said almost whining.

i cleared my throat and looked back at my food "let's forget this topic for now." i said and continued with my food.

"awww main maasi ban jaungi?" pari said laughing and i could feel the heat rush to my cheeks.

"pari if you say one more word i will take your phone and you'll be grounded for a month." i said and she stopped laughing and mumbled 'hitler' in her breath which i heard.

i finished my breakfast and got up to go upstairs and ayaansh followed shortly after.

he was still laughing.

"why are you even laughing? it's not funny." i said as we went towards the library.

"trust me, it was very funny." he said and earned only a kick on his foot again as he slowed down groaning in pain.

i am happy that for the first time we were not arguing.

we reached the library and i opened the door only to be welcomed by dust roaming around.

"yahaan par koi aaya nahi kya?" ansh asked and i coughed waving the dust off.

"yahaan bas papa hi aate the and main toh 3 saal se yahaan thi bhi nahi toh i don't think koi aaya hoga..." i said and coughed again "and main jab tak kuch bolun na tab tak toh safai karne ka kasht koi karega hi nahi." i said and opened another door in the library which had the old physical copies and documents.

"okay.... so where do we start from?" ansh asked as we looked at the 20 huge boxes in front of us which had about hundreds of files.

"let's call for some help." i said and he nodded calling vihaan and pari.

as soon as pari entered followed by Vihaan, both of them started coughing because of the dust.

"holy shit. we have to look through all of these?" Vihaan asked and i nodded sheepishly as all of us sat down browsing through the files.

about four hours later and countless death threats we gave to each other i finally found something.

"guys i think i found it." i said and all of them settled on either sides of me.

"Omkar Srivastav, age 34, hired:25th november 2015, Fired:15th september 2021..." i browsed through the details and found an address with a phone number.

"I tried calling this number through the anonymous one and it's invalid." Vihaan said looking at his laptop.

"But i do know something..." Ansh said and i looked at him. He looked.. ..afraid?

"what is it?" i asked him and he took a deep breath.

"This guy is responsible for your parent's death and the threats which the other man gave, one thing is for sure." he said looking hesitant and i looked at pari and Vihaan who seemed to understand what he was trying to say but i was still clueless.

"Isha he is going to try to kill you at a public event." he said and i let out a sigh. i am not gonna die this easily.

"and the only 'public' event i know right now is your wedding." pari said and i smiled.

"what is brewing in your mind right now?" ansh asked looking at me with a horrified expression and my smile grew wider.

"if he wants to kill me... why don't we let him try?" i said and their eyes widened.

"NO!" all of them said in unision.

"guys... do you really think i'm gonna die that easily..." i said and they were shaking their heads furiously.

"no isha this is not fucking happening-""are you out of your fucking mind ishu-""bhabhi, no offense but i thought you were smart-"

all of them were blabbering as their voices were getting in my head giving me a goddamn headache.

do they really think i am taking this decision impulsively?

"Enough! i thought about it and that is why i am doing it so i don't find any point of argument here."i said and all of them went silent still looking at me with questioning eyes.

"par ishu ek baar-" pari began and oh god please give me patience.

(god- nope!)

"preksha! end of discussion." i said walking out of the library.

i heard footsteps running behind me and someone grabbed my wrist pulling me back.

i collided with Ansh. My hands went on his shoulders as an instinct and he put his arm around me, balancing me.

his hair were all messed up with a few strands falling on his beautiful face. i am one thousand percent sure that god took extra time to make him. why the fuck was he so hot-

no. nononono... ishani you cannot think like that about him at all. i shook the weird thoughts away trying to pull myself back but he just tightened his hold around me pulling me closer.

does this guy have any idea about how him being this close to me is doing this weird tingling feeling in my heart?

"i'm not letting you take this risk Isha" he said pulling me back from my chain of thoughts.

"it's not a risk ansh, i know what i am doing and i am just not going to have security on me baaki sab toh safe hi rahenge..." i tried to reason but he just put his finger on my lips shutting me up.

butterflies. that's all i can say to explain what i am feeling right now.

"no. we are not taking this risk and that is final." he said making me sigh.

bipolar bitch.

calm down Isha. for the first time in years you are being nice to each other so don't ruin it.

"ansh... nothing will happen and anyways zyada se zyada kya hoga? i'm gonna get shot or something. that's it. don't worry i'm not gonna die before making you regret your decision of marrying me." i said jokingly, ruffling his already messed up hair and placing a kiss on his cheek.

he's blushing.

i saw him blush after i kissed him on the cheek!!!!!

i walked away biting back a smile and he was just rooted at his spot.

Ayaansh Yaduvanshi being flustered? Interesting...

If he can be bipolar then so can I.

The game is on baby.

Pari was sitting on my bed with an angry face, glaring at me.

"sorry." i said looking at her with a sad smile.

she didn't reply and just looked at the other side.

"sorry pari" i said hugging her and she made an angry face but hugged me back.

"please don't do it na ishu." she tried to convince me again but i looked at her and made her sit on the bed, taking a seat beside her.

"if i do it then we might have a chance to catch the person who is trying to kill me." i reasoned holding her hand.

"what if something happens to you? i'll die if something happened to you!" she said and looked at me with teary eyes.

Her crying was my biggest weakness. I always pampered her like the princess she was and she rarely cried. One exception was 2 years ago when she left her college in New York and returned back to India. She cried a lot one night and she never told me the reason even if i tried to find it out.

"pari...baccha don't cry.... nothing will happen to me!" i said and she sniffled wiping her tears.

"you won't leave me right?" she asked trying to control her tears. There is some other reason.

"what happened? something is definitely wrong pari and if i find that person who made you cry i'll just murder them straight away." i said and she shook her head hugging me.

"please just tell me you won't leave me." she said and i caressed her hair "i'll never leave you."

she pulled back wiping off her tears.

"now tell me what happened?" i asked as she shook her head with a fake smile "kuch nahi... maybe my periods are near that's why i'm high on emotions"

lie. She could lie to anyone in this world but me. I could see straight through her lies...

"acha you tell me... after you left jiju ran behind you, what did you talk about?" she tried to change the topic and i let her. if she doesn't want to talk about it then i won't force her.

one thing about preksha is that you never force her to do anything!

"ok fine i'll tell you..." i finally gave in to her demands.

"ok so is it cute or is it spicy??" she asked wiggling her brows.

"i made ansh blush!" i said and her jaw dropped.

"YOU WHAT???" she said jumping on the bed and took out a packet of chips from my drawer.

i knew that we will be spending the next one hour analyzing the words and expressions of the situation...

"i made The Ayaansh Yaduvanshi blush!" i said and she jumped again asking me to tell her everything.

"so... after i left he came in the corridor..."

Early updateeeeeeeeee

today ayaansh was a little...

follow me on instagram for reels and updates: tithi._

acha okay i love you byeee

8. Hope

[Ishani's pov...]

Am I happy?

no.

today is my haldi ceremony. Almost everyone gets happy when their wedding functions start. But it's not the same for me. I know this caring side of his is just a facade. I know he will never change.

I know he will hurt me. I know he can never forgive me even if i never had a choice.

but, I just hope it doesn't hurt much. Just not too much. I've already had enough. Just not too much.

"kahaan kho gayi?"pari asked me while putting a bindi on my forehead, pulling me out of my thoughts.

"kuch nahi." i said and she narrowed her eyes at me.

"jiju ke baare mein soch rahi hai?" she said wiggling her eyebrows.

"yes. but not in the way you are expecting me to." i said and she rolled her eyes.

"hayeeee... nazar na lage tujhe!" she said while putting kajal behind my ear.

"acha by the way veer is also coming today." she said and my eyes widened in shock.

i really really hope that she is joking.

"you're joking right?" i asked her and she shook her head with a smile.

"why would you do that preksha? why would you call my ex-boyfriend to my wedding!" i yelled at her and she laughed as if it was the funniest thing ever.

"okay before you say anything else, let me remind you that he is also our business partner before your ex-boyfriend." she said and i paced in my room while she was just laughing her ass off.

"toh main use reception party mein bula rahi thi na? tune use saare functions ka invite bhej diya?" i said and she nodded enthusiastically.

"are ishu there were two reasons number one, he should know that he lost everything by cheating. and second, i wanted jiju to be jealous." she said and i let out a humorous chuckle and the second part.

"i know ayaansh and i know that he won't be jealous." i said and checked myself in the mirror.

damn. i'm hot.

[ishani's outfit...]

"we'll see about that." she said with a smirk pulling me out of the room.

i moved in the garden where everyone was already present including ayaansh.

maybe i should not think this but fuck... he looks freaking hot in that kurta.

i sat beside him on a haldi stool.

"it's rude to stare isha..." he whispered and that's when i realized that i was checking him out.

"i am rude." i said and he just shook his head with a sigh.

I could feel him checking me out when i looked away.

after a few minutes Dadisa came and gave us blessings.

"i hope ki tumhara jeevan khushiyon se bhara ho aur koi bhi problem na aye. tum dono humesha sukhi raho aur ek dusre se bohot pyaar karo..." she said and wanted to laugh at her statement.

i wanted to laugh at myself for hoping that it will ever happen.

but instead i just smiled and she applied a little haldi on our faces.

"veer aagaya..." pari whispered in my ear with a chuckle while i just glared at her.

"usko yahaan se dur rakh... main kya intro dungi? 'Hi veer this is my fiance ayaansh and ayaansh this is my ex-boyfriend veer'." i mocked with a sarcastic smile while she just smiled and walked away.

maa and papa came and smudged haldi on our faces.

"ishani tum humari beti jaisi ho and trust me we'll take care of you. I know you miss your parents but we will make sure that you feel like we are your parents." maa said with a smile and tears well up in my eyes but i didn't let them fall.

ayaansh interwind his fingers with mine and i looked at him.

"it's okay... your parents must be happy." he whispered and i nodded my head with a small smile.

"and you..." his father pointed at ayaansh with a serious expression "take care of ishani or else i will beat you to death."

"don't worry... i will take care of her my dear father." liar. what a bloody liar.

as soon as they left after applying haldi other cousins and relatives start coming in. my hands and cheeks were filled with haldi but my heart was as empty as a dark room.

there was one thing which was eating me alive.

hope.

"looks like the drama is here...." pari said in my ear and i followed her gaze to see veer coming towards us.

That's when i realized that i was still holding ayaansh's hand and this guy didn't even realize.

veer came in front of me with a smile....a sad smile?

he took haldi from the bowl and applied it on my face. His hand lingered on my face a little longer than it would be considered appropriate.

he gave a small smile and moved back.

ayaansh withdrawed his hand from mine and cupped my jaw making me face him.

he wiped of the haldi from my face which was applied by veer.

"what are you doing?" i asked him as he cleaned his hand with a towel and took haldi from the bowl near him.

"telling him that you are already taken." he said and smudged the haldi on my cheeks then he kissed my forehead.

HE KISSED MY FUCKING FOREHEAD!!!!!

ew. why am i acting like a teenage girl who got her first crush?

BUT HE KISSED MY FOREHEAD!!!

"jealous much?" I said in an attempt to ease the tension lingering between us.

"in your dreams." he said with a sarcastic smile.

"trust me you would not like to know my dreams." i whispered winking at him.

He blushed.

i want to laugh.

He freaking blushed. his face was a deep shade of red before he cleared his throat.

" i mean i don't blame you... i am the kind of person that people would dream about..." he said smirking at me.

shit he pulled out an uno reverse.

"joke of the decade." i scoffed and he looked at me offended.

"oh hello! ladkiyan marti hain mujhpe." he said looking at me as if i just accused him of a murder.

"tum par marti nahi hain! tumhe dekh kar mar jaati hai! kaisi chimpanzee si shakal hai." i said flipping my hair off my shoulder.

"moye moye." vihaan said from behind us and i bursted out laughing.

"Very funny." ansh said and gave a sarcastic smile.

i stopped laughing after a few seconds to look at ansh who was already looking at me. Not even looking he was....gazing at me.

fuck why am i blushing? i could feel the heat rush to my face as he looked at me.

"it's rude to stare ansh..." i said mirroring his words from before.

"it's not rude to stare someone who belongs to me..." he said and i am blushing.

i looked away and it's good that there is haldi on my face otherwise my face would've been visibly red.

---

i was looking for pari after the function.

"pari! where is my phone yaar?" i asked her slightly annoyed.

"jiju ke paas hai!" she said and was about to go the other way before i stopped her again.

"and tere jiju kahaan hai?" i asked her with an annoyed smile.

"are tera pati hai toh tujhe hi pata hoga na? mujhe kya pata?" she said and ran in the other direction.

ugh! where the hell is this asshole?

i turned back and bumped into someone. i looked up to see veer who had a slight smile on his face.

i moved back a few steps to create a distance between us and he spoke up" how are you Isha?"

That name sounded weird in his voice.

I am Isha only for ansh!! my inner voice mocked but i shook the thoughts away.

"first of all, don't call me that. and second of all it's none of your business." i said in my usual cold demeanor as i would talk to my client.

"I'm sorry Ishani." he said and i wanted to laugh but maintained my face in an expressionless one.

"for what? for cheating on me or for being here?" i said and he wanted to say something

"for bot-"

"you know what? bolo hi mat i don't care. I would've cancelled our deal too but preksha and vikram ne bohot mehnat ki thi uspe that's why i'm tolerating you." i said and he was about to say something when i felt a hand on my waist.

I looked up to see ansh who shook hands with veer.

fuck, it's gonna be awkward. calm down.

"Nice to meet you mr?" he said and i knew that the his grip on veer's hand was very tight. tight enough to cramp the bones.

"veer mittal. Nice to meet you too Mr. Yaduvanshi..." veer said after pulling his hand back from the handshake.

"let's go Isha we have work right?" ansh said and god i was so greatful for him to be there.

"Umm- yeah let's go." i said and before we could leave , veer left the place.

i let out a relieved sigh.

i wanted to move knowing the conversation i'll be having with ansh right now.

i tried to walk away but he pulled me back and i collided with his chest. The way he was looking at me made me feel as if thousands of golden bubbles were dancing in my stomach.

he twirled my hair and put them behind my ear.

shit, i want to kiss him right now.

no. nonono what the hell is wrong with your thoughts ishani.

"who was he Ishani?" Why would he call me Ishani? I am only Isha for him!

"somebody...nobody." i said fumbling with my words. him being this close to me was not helping at all. i was melting more and more into his touch and god help me i don't want to leave.

he pulled me even closer. fuck i'll kiss him.

nonononono... what are you even thinking?!?!

"don't lie to me Ishani." he said in a stern voice but his tone tone was still soft.

"he was a business client... and also my ex boyfriend. Pari invited him just because she wanted to make him regret his decision of cheating on me..." i said he sighed. Was it a frustrated sigh or a relieved one? i don't know.

"tell him to stay away from you..." he said in a calm voice. was everything okay? he never spoke calmly with me.

"stop giving me hope ansh..." i finally said it and he just gave me a small smile before leaning in and placing a kiss on my cheek.

i am definitely red by now.

then the other cheek and my forehead.

"i am not giving you false hopes Isha... I am just doing what I am doing." he said and connected his forehead with mine.

if this is what peace feels like... then i want to stay like this forever.

i don't care anymore if this is just an act or not.

if this is what being wanted feels like then i am ready for any false hope.

----

so....... hehehehehe(main pagal ho gayi hoon)

what do you think are the feelings real or false?

for reels and updates follow me on instagram: tithi._

love youuuuuuuu

9.Love

He was crying. He was crying because of me.

I broke his trust. I broke his fucking trust and won't even blame him if he doesn't ever forgive me.

"Go away Isha before i say something which I'll regret." he said and wiped his tears from the back of his hand.

"I didn't have a choice ayaansh, i tried to fix it but it turned out totally different-" I tried to say but he left my hand with a jerk.

"does it matter?" he asked still not looking at me in my eyes.

I deserve it.

"Ansh they had my parents at gunpoint..." i said cupping his jaw making him look at me. The anger was clear in his eyes, he took my hand off his face and twisted my wrist.

It was so fucking painful but i knew he was angry, because of me.

"No need to give any more of your excuses because they are dead now. They are not here with me and i will never forgive you for that." he said and my wrist hurt even more.

"Can you just listen to me for once? It was a do or die situation for me, i couldn't do anything!" I said trying to be as calm as i can but his words and actions weren't letting me be calm.

he left my wrist and i was pushed up against the wall.

"what were you so scared of?" he asked me finally looking in my eyes with so much hate.

I had no answer. I was speechless and words were not making there way out of my throat.

he let out a humorous chuckle and i knew there was no going back. I deserve this hate from him.

"No answer? that's what i expected." he said "i'm sorry ansh please-" i tried to say but he just walked out slamming the door shut.

Tears left my eyes which i had been controlling for long time.

I looked at my wrist which was now turning blue but it didn't hurt as much as my heart hurt right now.

I messed up, pretty fucking bad. I hurt him.

I fucking hate myself.

...

present.

"mam it's done." The henna artist said and i snapped out of my thoughts.

"umm- yeah okay. thank you." i said and she got up to leave.

The mehendi function was going on and everyone was applying henna on their hands.

"this is so damn pretty..." Pari said looking at my mehendi and placing a kiss on my cheek.

"very much unlike you." Vikram said from beside pari and i glared at him "zyada zubaan nahi chal rahi teri!"

"bhagwaan ne zubaan di hai toh istemaal karne mein kya jaa raha hai?" he said with a sarcastic smile.

"aur main ye zubaan kaat bhi sakti hoon toh it's better if you shut up." I said and he raised his hands in surrender and he pulled out a chair for pari.

As pari was about to sit down suddenly Vihaan appeared from behind grabbing her hand.

"bhabhi your mehendi looks amazing but i really need to talk to Preksha right now..." he said and dragged pari away from there.

i noticed pari's expression change before she walked away with him., she was not too happy, she looked...sad and tired?Was Vihaan the reason that she looked so drained out from a few days? What the hell is going on with her? What did he do?

"Isko kya hua?" Vikram asked and i shrugged my shoulders.

[Ayaansh's pov...]

Walking through the corridor i accidentally bumped with someone, i opened my mouth to apologize but closed it as soon as I saw him.

Shitij Rajwansh.

"Hi Ayaansh... apni biwi ko dekhne jaa rahe ho?" he asked and i internally rolled my eyes.

He was so fucking annoying.

"Tumse matlab?" I asked with a smile and he rolled his eyes as i walked away.

"waise agar nahi mil rahe ho toh mil lo kyonki pata chale ki jab tum naa ho tab kisi aur ke saath rang raliyaan mana rahi ho meri behen." he said and i ignored his words walking downstairs.

Is it right? Me pretending to fall for her just to break her...

Ishani was the kind of woman who can bring any guy to his knees.

But she made many fucking mistakes. A lot of them.

If it was anything else i would've forgiven her but it wasn't just a small mistake.

They died because of her.

My grandparents and my sister died because of her.

Only if she wasn't so scared at that time, they would've been okay, they would've been with me right now.

Ishani was my everything a few years ago. She was my best friend, my therapist, my life, my fucking everything.

I believed her, I trusted her, I was devoted to her, I loved her.

I fucking loved her but she broke me.

loved. I don't love her anymore. She was once my everything but now she is nothing to me.

I got in the garden where the ceremony was going on and looked at her.

If I didn't hate her this much then i would've definitely been dead by her beauty.

She was talking to a guy... her PA?

A smile was on her face and they both were laughing. Why was she laughing with him? was he that funny?

I walked over to her taking a seat beside her.

"This is beautiful..." I said looking at her hands filled with henna.

"Thank you..." she said with a smile adorning her face. She was still unsure of everything.

"acha mujhe kuch poochna tha..." she said and i raised my eyebrows at her.

"is everything okay with pari and vihaan... i mean they don't seem okay." This woman's own love life is at stake and she is worried about her sister's love life?? I am marrying a crazy person.

"I don't know... Vihaan never told me anything about them. All I know is that they were friends." I said and she tilted her head looking at pari.

" 'were' is the keyword here because they were friends, then they didn't talk to each other for years and now suddenly they want to have 'private' conversations? this is bullshit. Preksha looks so freaking drained out now-a-days" she said and turned her head towards me. "If i find out that your brother made my sister cry then i will bury him alive and main ye bhool jaaungi ki wo mera devar hai!" she said in one go.

Damn, she looks hot when she's angry.

What the fuck am i thinking? I shook off my not-so-holy thoughts and looked at her again.

"okay angry young woman calm down... Vihaan will not hurt her in any way. I know him and i don't think that he'll ever do something like that." I know Vihaan, I know he'll never hurt her.

"okay forget about this and tell me... what did you do yesterday after haldi?" I tried to make a conversation like a loving, caring and nice husband that i am. (note the sarcasm)

"ummm... i had some work so i went to office in the afternoon then aane ke baad main pari ke saath bahar gayi thi fir i completed the book which i was reading." She said with a smile and i nodded wile taking the plate a servant gave me.

Taking rice in a spoon i forwarded it towards her mouth and she looked at the spoon then at me.

oh... i forgot she still didn't trust me.

"khaalo i know ki kuch nahi khaya hai subah se. What a careless person are you Isha." i said and she opened her mouth eating it.

"Tell me about the book." i said because i saw her smile widen when she told me that she read a book.

"you really want to know?" she asked me with narrowed eyes and i nodded giving her another bite.

"It was such a great book and the main characters were just chef's kiss. it's a series you know, 'folk of the air'. The FML was such a badass..." she just kept on ranting about the book while i kept on feeding her the food. She looked so pure and happy in the moment that i almost forgot that we could never be anything.

I can't fall for her.

Not again.

Yup.... Our Ayaansh is a broken baby...

Sorry for the chota sa chapter but next chapter i promise bada dungi

for reels and updates, follow me on instagram: tithi._

i love youuu

10. Scared

[Ishani's pov...]

5 Years ago...

"Tumhara dimaag kharaab hai kya ayaansh? lag jayegi haath pe." I said to ayaansh who was trying to detangle my bracelet which was stuck in the wire fence. It got stuck when we were walking past it.

"Are kuch nahi hoga Isha why are you so tensed all the time- Ow!" he said but his hand got a cut because of the sharp wire.

"Isliye humesha tensed rehti hoon main! get back and leave it." i said trying to pull him back but he just wouldn't budge and finally took out the bracelet.

"see i told you i'm the best in everything." he said while i just glared at him.

"kisi aur se bhi naikalwa sakte the na?" i said as he took my hand and tied the bracelet around my wrist.

"kisi aur ko bhi lag jaati na and anyways this was my gift which got stuck so it was my job to get it out." he said and kissed my wrist.

"kaise kaise kaam karte ho tum..." i said and took his hand and thank god it was not some huge cut.

"Isha meri jaan you have no idea what i can actually do for you." he said and hugged me.

This was peace. This was calm. This was comfort.

I kept my head on his chest hearing his heartbeats. It felt like music to my ears.

I love him.

...

present

I looked at the bracelet on my hand. Ayaansh gifted it to me on my birthday 5 years ago.

I loved him but I broke him.

And I fucking hate myself for it.

A lone tear escaped my eye thinking about the last good day of my life but i was quick to wipe it when i heard a knock.

I opened the door and got out smiling at Ansh.

"Are you sure that she'll know something?" He asked me as we walked downstairs.

We were going to the address where Omkar Srivastav used to live. From the information we have, we know that there was a caretaker for his 10 year old son and no one else.

"I hope so..." I said and we moved out of the house.

"What if you die? There are literally people out there who thirsty for your blood..." He said and i chuckled at his horrified expression.

"I won't die this easily." I said and he opened the passenger door for me.

If we are correct then we might find something there and if we don't then there is a high chance that both of us might end up dead.

after 30 minutes we reached the house which was on the outskirts of the city. I checked my hair and makeup in the car mirror and Ansh just looked at me as if i am a ghost.

"You know you can end up dead right?" He asked and i nodded touching up by lip gloss.

"And you are checking your makeup?" He asked again and i nodded.

"I should look pretty if i die." I said and he got out opening my door.

It was a huge house, no doubt he was a minister but why was it situated outside the city?

I rang the bell about 3 times but nobody opened so i signaled the guard behind us to break the door.

As soon as we got inside we were met my darkness and a bloody foul smell.

"take this." Ansh said giving me is handkerchief and taking one for himself from the guard behind us to cover our noses.

It smells disgusting.

"Check inside and tell us if you find something." Ansh said and the guards dispersed into different sections of the house.

"This place is horrible." I said and opened the window looking outside with my gun in hand.

i felt something click behind me and i immediately turned behind pointing my gun at their head.

It was woman who looked very, very familiar. She had her gun pointed at my head. I heard another click and saw ansh beside her with his gun pointed at the woman's head.

"ooo.. protective husband i see..." she said and put her hand back down but i still had my gun pointed at her head.

"oh come on guys don't tell me you don't recognize me..." she said with a pout and she looked even more familiar.

"we don't recognize you at all..." ayaansh said and she rolled her eyes.

"really mere makkhan aur malai?" she said and my eyes widen at the nickname.

this can't be her.

"What the actual fuck?" ansh whispered and we both looked at her with widened eyes.

"Rashmi motherfucking Rai" I said and we both lowered our hands still in the shock.

Our best friend, Rashmi Rai who went to london and did not have any contact with us at all.

This bitch.

Her eyes widened as i opened my heel and threw it at her and it hit her on her shoulder.

"kutti." Ayaansh said and she smiled sheepishly.

"kamini." i said and she backed off a little before i could punch her.

"kalyug ki pootna.""gadhi ki bachi.""south pole ki suar.""chipkali."

We were constantly yelling at her but she just smiled and before we could say anything else she got us in a group hug.

6 bloody years. All of us were back together after 6 bloody years.

"wait wait wait wait.... what are you doing here?" i asked her that before any conversation.

she smiled and took out her ID card "Rashmi Rai Chowdhari, Senior Narcotics Agent, Reporting ma'am." she said and I glared at her again.

I wanted to say a lot of things but before i begin she cut me off "We can do the shouting later but right now I'm on duty." she began and ansh raised his eyebrow asking her to continue.

"Your life is in danger and i am assigned to look into this." She said in all seriousness and concern in her voice.

"As if we didn't know that earlier..." ansh said and she led us in a room where the guards were circling something.

"This might be disturbing but you need to see this." She said and the guards moved away.

I had to look away because the sight was too much.

I hate this. I want to get out of here.

There were two dead bodies in there. A 10 year old boy and a grown up woman. Their entrails lurching out with dried blood all around. Their bodies were decomposing and this was the reason for that horrible smell. But what shook me was a a note, written with blood on the wall.

'The next person will be you, our beloved Rani Sa.'

"Bury the bodies." I said before getting out of the house.

It was not like I was scared of blood or bodies, Most of the time I was the one sending people to hell. I just hated to see innocent people dying. It made me sick to the core.

I never get scared. Nobody wants a queen who gets scared but this time i was scared. I was scared to the deepest part of my heart.

Those bodies, the note, it was a warning.

I got out of the house and took a few deep breaths.

"Isha..." I heard his voice behind me and i turned around.

"I-I just felt-" I said but he just wrapped his arms around me pulling me into a hug.

"I know Isha. You don't have to explain yourself." He said and i hugged him back. He caressed my hair as i put my head on his chest hearing his heartbeat.

His heartbeat was my favorite music a few years ago.

Maybe it still is my favorite.

"Once we find who did this i'll kill them." He said and hugged me closer to him, running his fingers through my hair.

"Okay... love birds no PDA in front of me... it's disgusting to see my best friends being all lovey dovey..." Rashmi said coming towards us.

I moved back and narrowed my eyes at her and ansh's hand was still over my shoulder.

"Get in the car you are going home with us." I said and she smiled getting in the car.

"Ishu... I'll find out who did that, don't worry i'm the best in my field." She said and i sat in the back with her.

"Main driver hoon kya jo dono peeche baith gaye ho?" Ansh said and i nodded motioning him to start the car as if he was actually my driver.

"Wait... how are you Rashmi Rai 'Chowdhari'?" ansh asked and started the car.

"oh... wo actually I kinda got married and have kid." She said it so casually as if it was nothing big.

"YOU WHAT??" we yelled together at her and she closed her ears.

"ghar pohonch ke batati hoon main tumhe sab." she said with a smile and after about 20 minutes we reached home.

I got out of the car but as soon as i did my heel twisted and so did my foot as i groaned in pain.

"How can you be so clumsy Isha?" ansh asked me while picking up as i squealed.

"are neeche utaro mujhe, pagal ho gaye ho kya? meri Dadisa bohot old-fashioned hain, kalesh kardengi wo ghar pe..." i said but he just carried me inside.

My Dadisa was one of those people who still believed that girls should get married as soon as they turned 21 and should remain shy and obedient.

"karne do kalesh agar karna hai toh... apni biwi ko uthane mein kaisi sharam?" he said and moved towards the entrance.

"Besharam Aadmi." I said but he ignored my comment.

"He bhagwaan! ye kya dekh lia!!" I heard the overdramatic voice of my Dadisa and gave an 'i told you so' look to ansh who just smiled and put me on the couch.

"Ouch lag rahi hai touch mat karo!" I said to maa who was trying to look at my foot.

"okay wait... this is just a slight twist toh if you just let me do something it will heal in a few hours..." Rashmi said and sat on the couch put my hand over my mouth to stop myself from screaming as she gave my foot a harsh twist.

"does it still hurt?" Ansh asked me as i tried to move my foot but winced as it still hurt a little.

"not as much, i think i'll survive.." i said and looked up to see everyone glaring at me.

"by the way who are you?" maa asked looking at rashmi. even she didn't recognize her.

"sach mein nahi pehchaan paa rahe aap log? itni badal gayi kya main?" she asked with a frown.

"teri shakal, akal aur himmat teeno badal gayi hai so you better explain yourself." I said and Rashmi turned her face back to everyone.

"It's me. Rashmi..." she said and everyone's jaw dropped.

I saw as pari took of her sandal and threw it at Rashmi "abe nahi yaar teri behen already peet chuki hai mujhe"

"so what are you expecting after disappearing into thin air?" maa said and she apologized thouroughly.

She was a sweetheart to everyone so they forgave her.

"Don't you dare." i said to ansh who was about to pick me up from the couch.

"oh i do dare." he said and picked me up.

"Mujhse nahi dekha jaa raha ye sab main jaa rahi hoon." Dadisa said walking away while I just closed my eyes in embarrassment.

He walked upstairs as Rasmi trailed behind us.

"why do you even care?" i mumbled and he sighed.

"even i don't know when i started caring Isha. But now that i do, there is no one who can care for you more than me, jaan." He said and i moved my face to the other side.

Jaan.

He called me Jaan after 5 years.

Rashmi opened the door and he made me sit on the bed.

"Explain." He said to Rashmi as she sat on the bed with us.

"After i left for London I started training as a Narcotics Agent. I wasn't able to contact you because I was undercover." she said and i nodded asking her to continue.

"I met Ariv there and fell in love with him. We got married 2 years ago and we have a daughter named Anshika. We both got transferred back to India a year ago and i was assigned for your investigation case." She completed and smiled.

"You have a daughter and i missed everything." I said and looked down. My best friend has a daughter and i missed everything.

"you did not miss anything idiot she's just 6 months old." she said and i sighed in relief.

"where is she?" ansh asked and i saw the smile widen as she talked about her daughter.

"with her dad. Today was there father-daughter day and they basically kicked me out of the house." she said and i laughed at her face.

ansh's phone rang and he picked it up.

"I have to leave, I'll be late, Meet you tomorrow at our wedding." he said, kissed my cheek and walked out of the room.

This guy does the most unexpected things at the most unexpected moments and leaves me as a blushing mess.

As soon as the door closed Rashmi asked me a question which i was not expecting.

"What's going on between you two? I am your best friend an i know when you two are telling the truth and when you are not."

i looked down not being able to meet her eye "this is a love marriage right? you two were completely in love with each other." she said and i shook my head trying to push back my tears.

"it's an arranged marriage. I..." i said and she made me look at her.

"ab bol, meri aankho mein dekh kar bol." she said and a tear escaped my eye.

"I messed up Rashmi, I fucking messed up and he hates me. But I still..." I tried to complete my sentence but a sob escaped my throat.

"complete the sentence, let it out Ishu." she said and hugged me.

"I can't pretend to hate him anymore. I just can't." i said and wiped my tears by the back of my hand.

"I still love him." I said and she nodded while ruffling my hair.

"I know you both. I know you both figure out a way because according to me, in your story Ayaansh will always fall in love with you in the end..."She said and I look at her in confusion.

"You think?" I asked and she patted my cheek.

"I know."

I love Ayaansh.

I love him so fucking much that it hurts.

Bola tha na bada update.... ye lo de diya.

For reels and updates follow me on instagram: tithi._

love youuuuuuuuuu

11. The Wedding

[Ishani's pov...]

"OMG she is so cuteee!!!!!" I said as i picked up Rashmi's daughter in my arms. She was so small and delicate. Just like a doll.

"She is a mixture of you both." Ansh said looking towards Rashmi and Ariv who were smiling.

"But I'm still mad at you." I said to Rashmi who looked at me with puppy eyes.

"I said sorry na...." She said looking sad.

"We decided to get married together... How dare you get married before me!" I said and I saw she looked panicked.

"Ummm... Ariv I think we should get divorced and get married again." Rashmi said to Ariv who looked at her with widened eyes.

"Are they always like this when they are together?" Ariv asked ansh who nodded.

"Yes they are." He said and I glared at him.

"Wait the main confusion is.... ki main ladke walon ki side se hoon ya fir ladki walon ki?" Rashmi said and i chuckled.

"Obviously ladki wali hai tu.""Obviously ladke wali hai tu."

both me and ansh said at the same time and were about to argue when the little girl in my arms stirred a little and let out a soft coo.

"awwwwww main mar jaungi itni cuteness se. Hi baby, I am your maasi and this is your mausa." I said as soon as the girl opened her eyes.

"Ummm... excuse me? I am her Mama and you are her Mami." Ansh said and i looked at him with my jaw dropped.

"Now the real war begins..." Ariv said while Rashmi just took the baby from my arms before she witnesses me killing ansh.

My phone chimed with a notification.

"Shit." I said and and ansh raised his eyebrows.

"Maa is asking me to get home and she is going to kill us if she finds out that we're together. She said it was some rasam ki hum log shaadi se pehle nahi mil sakte." I said and we ran towards the car to get home before maa actually kills us.

....

[Ayaansh's pov...]

6 years ago...

She is so beautiful.

She looks so beautiful when she is reading with her hair messed up and glasses on her eyes. Just so damn beautiful.

pata nahi kitne somvaar ke vrat rakhe the jo ise roz dekh pata hoon.

Well this is who I am right now, a teenager in love. Might sound stupid but god how can someone not fall for her.

I am completely, utterly, hopelessly, crazily in love with my Isha.

"Quesion 5 ka kya answer hai?" She asked me bringing me out of my lala land.

"ummm... Mitochondria." I said without thinking and she smiled.

"We're studying Geography, Ansh." She said with a smile on her face.

I am ready to become the biggest Idiot in the world if it brings a smile to her face.

She focused back on the book and then it clicked me that her father asked me to tell her something.

"Jaan?"

"Hmm?" She hummed in response her focus still not shifting from the book.

"Shitij is getting married. He thinks that maybe he'll get the throne after this." I said and she smiled again.

"Haan halwa hai na jo sabme baat te chale hum... My papa is way too smart to fall for these tricks of his. I'm feeling sorry for the girl whose getting married to him." She said and closed the book, finally giving me the attention I was craving.

"Agar tumne padhna start nahi kiya na toh pakka fail ho jaoge!" she said hitting me with the book.

"Ayaansh Yaduvanshi never fails, Isha madam." I said only to receive another smack.

"I'll marry you one day." I blurted out and she smiled widely at me.

"First of all, how are you so sure that I'll marry you? aur bhi bohot ladke ho sakte hain line mein." She said and I frowned at the question.

"I am sure because you know me... Kisi aur ladke ko bhatakne bhi nahi dunga tumhaare aas paas." I said as a wave of possessiveness washed over my heart.

"Okay then lover boy.... I'll marry you one day." She said and a smile bade it's way on my face.

.....

present

looks like i kept my word.

I'm marrying her.

I'm marrying the woman i was once in love with.

I'm marrying Ishani Rajwansh.

My thoughts came to a halt when a slow bridal entry song started playing and the huge door opened.

I hate to say this but wow.

She was beautiful.

She was always beautiful.

I put my hand forward and noticed the hesitation in her eyes before she took it and i helped her to get up.

She looked at me and i gulped looking at those eyes.

Those eyes.

Those hazel brown eyes which i once fell for.

They still hold that fire and hope.

The rose petals rain over us as she put the flower garland around my neck and I did the same.

Don't fall for her again. That's what i promised myself.

We sat at the pavilion and the priest started chanting the Mantras. I wasn't even focused on what he was saying. I was just focused on the woman sitting beside me.

I was marrying her. I was keeping my promise.

We stood up for the pheras and with each round i knew that i was changing my life completely. Each round meant that she will be there by my side as my wife.

Forever.

The priest asked me to tie the Mangalsutra around her neck.

I put my hands around her tying it and our noses touched while doing so. Her eyes met mine and that's when i realized that she was the most beautiful woman ever.

I took the sindoor in the coin and shifted her maangtika a bit, filling her hairline. A little sindoor fell on her nose and she looked at me not breaking the eye contact this time.

For the first time in my life i was not able to read her emotions.

It was done.

She was my wife now.

....

"Bhabhi you have to win. Bhai ka ego todna padega aaj." Vihaan said looking at Isha who chuckled at his words.

Both of us were sitting on stools facing each other with a bowl containing milk, vermllion and rose petals.

"Ishu give me the ring." Preksha said to Isha who slipped her engagement ring off her finger and preksha dipped it in the bowl mixing it.

"The one who finds the ring first will have the upper hand in marriage." Maa said and on the count of three both of us started finding the ring.

After about 30 seconds i found it and was about to pull it out but she held my hand inside the bowl.

"Give me the ring..." Isha whispered so only i can listen to her.

"No." I whispered back but she didn't leave my hand.

I looked up at her, she smiled and winked at me making me choke on air.

I coughed and my hold on the ring loosened and she took it.

bloody cheater.

"I win." She said pulling out the ring and everyone cheered.

"You cheated." I said and she smiled at me again.

"And how did I cheat ansh?" She asked as if she was the most innocent person in the world.

"you-you..." I tried to say something but gave up making everyone laugh.

[Ishani's pov...]

Marrying the person you love must be a great feeling right?

For me it's not.

I got married to the person I love but he doesn't love me at all.

He hates me.

The water was flowing on my head as i relaxed under the warm shower.

I should not be in love with him but I am and it hurts.

Sometimes I wish I could just turn off my emotions so I don't get hurt.

Getting out of the shower I changed into my night dress preparing myself to go to bed.

I opened the door to get out of the wardrobe and was greeted by my husband.

My husband.

"Hi wifey." He greeted with a smirk and god how much I wish to wipe that smirk of his face.

"Don't call me that." I said before taking out extra pillows from the cupboard and making a wall with them to divide the bed in two parts.

"What are you doing?" He asked me frowning.

"Dare to cross this line and I will cut your hand off." I said he chuckled while sitting down on the other side of the bed.

"You are my wife Isha... I have an all access pass to touch you any time I want to." He said getting up and moving closer to me.

"why did I even marry you? Now I regret breaking up with Veer. Just imagine how nice it would sound. Ishani Veer Mittal huh?" At this point I was just testing his patience and I knew I was succeeding in doing so.

"Oh really?" He said moving one step forward and I took one step back.

One step Forward and one step back. This continued till my back touched the wall and he was way too close to me.

So freaking close that his breath touched my face and my heartbeats picked up pace.

"Ishani. Ayaansh. Yaduvanshi." He said emphasizing each and every word and if he comes one step closer i will kiss him without any regrets.

"This is your name. I dare you to say your name with some other man and he will be 6 feet under the ground." He said his lips were millimeters away from mine.

"You are my wife Isha. Do you get it?" He said and right now my mind was in a haze and my body was going numb.

"You don't-" i tried to say but he put his finger on my lips.

"I don't want riddles, Isha. Answer the question. do. you. get it?" He said and I didn't even know why I gave in to his question "yes."

"Good. Everyone should know that you belong to me." He said and my mind was going completely against me. Why was it so hot in here?

"You're mine to touch," he said grazing his fingers over my arm making my breath hitch and goosebumps rise on my arm.

"Mine to kiss," he said and his lips brush over mine. It was not even a kiss just a slight brush still my body went numb and my heartbeats moved in the highest speed possible.

"And most definitely mine to fuck." He said and his lips finally connect with mine. I was pinned against the wall and his hands went on my waist pulling me closer.

My hands went behind his back and moved upwards to his hair tugging them eliciting a groan. My mind and body both were against me at the moment. At this rate my heart will explode.

He bit on my lower lip and I gasped due to the pain. He seized the moment and slipped his tongue in my mouth. The next thing I know is that I was pushed on the bed with him hovering over me still kissing.

His tongue explored my mouth tasting every inch. I never wanted this moment to end. It felt like heaven. Him being so close to me felt like heaven. After a few seconds he broke the kiss and my head fell back as his mouth fell to neck.

He kissed down my jaw to my neck and my collarbone and i let out a hiss as he bit on my neck.

A moan escaped my lips as he sucked on the part where he just bit and lapped it with his tongue to ease the sting.

Kissing up my neck to my jaw and back to my lips he pecked me a few times and then looked in my eyes.

Heat rushed to my cheeks and my mind became foggy with my breaths heavy as he brushed my hair out of face.

"I haven't even done anything yet you are so breathless Isha... What will happen when I actually do something?" He said and kissed my neck and my face a few times before getting up.

"Go to sleep, jaan or else I'll actually do something to make you breathless." He said and walked inside the washroom.

I sat up on my bed with just one thing going on in my mind.

What the fuck just happened?

I was just trying to test his patience and it lead to a freaking make out session?

There is no going back.

There is no chance that i will fall out of love.

I love him way too much.

----

ummmm.............. okay.

You have to agree that Ayaansh is hot.

I am screaming and kicking my feet in the air.

chalo I'll meet you next time tab tak ke liye bye bye.

for reels and updates follow me on Instagram : tithi._

love youuuuuuuuuuuu

12. Those Eyes

I had to update this chapter again because it needed heavy editing.

those who read it before can skip if needed.

[Ayaansh's's pov...]

I woke up with someone throwing a pillow on my face.

fuck, I'm married now.

"Kya hai isha?" I woke up groggily. sleep was still in my eyes.

"Agar aapne apni beauty sleep poori kar li ho toh uth jaiye patidev.... and please check the time!" She said and yelled at the last part.

"What even is the time- WHAT THE FUCK?" i jumped out of the bed after looking at the clock.

9:00 AM.

"Why didn't wake me up?" I said running towards the washroom stumbling on my way.

"Maine theka le rakha hai tumhe uthane ka? Are main pichle aadhe ghante se saree pehnne ka try kar rahi thi mere dimaag mein nahi aya ki tum exist karte ho!" She said and that's when i took a proper look at her.

holy shit.

beautiful.

She was so fucking beautiful.

That red saree on her made her look even more beautiful.

The kajal in her eyes enhancing the color of them.

Those eyes.

They had the mixed combination of brown and hazel. As if sands on the beach are shining in the sunlight.

Those dreamy eyes who were once full of life.

They are now empty. But they still have a hint of innocence and purity in them. So pure that I didn't want to hurt her at all.

I feel like I would drown in them and never come back.

Sometimes my heart tells me to love her again but... I can't.

That gold choker in her neck and the earrings in her ears made her look complete.

And that Mangalsutra. Utterly beautiful.

fuck, I'm going crazy.

I came out of my thoughts when she spoke again .

"If you are done admiring me, then please go inside the washroom." she said with a fake smile and I just shook my head going inside.

pretending to be in love with her is going to be hard.

Because I know there is a huge risk that i might actually fall in love with her.

again.

And that is my biggest nightmare.

To get my heart broken again.

To lose someone close to me again.

To lose her again.

No. No, I can't let this overpower me.

Before I could guilt trip myself even more the flashes of last night came in my mind.

I kissed her.

Only I know how much I was craving to do that.

Not my fault she was looking way too pretty last night to even control my inner urges.

She always looks pretty to you dude. My conscience mocked me and I took a deep breath

----

Walking downstairs and entering the Living room, I found Isha whining about something while Dadisa had a stern expression mustered on her face.

My parents and Chachi were trying not to laugh while Pari and Vihaan were no where to be seen.

Where the hell is Vihaan when I need him?

I walked over to the table and touched the feet of all the elders.

"but why? Mera hi ghar hai! apne hi ghar mein kon pehli rasoi ki rasam karta hai?" Isha whined and i bit my lip trying not to laugh.

"saaf saaf bol do ki tumhe khaana banana nahi aata." I whispered to her much to her annoyance.

"Are rasam toh rasam hi hoti hai na?Karni padegi!" Dadisa said again and a chuckle escaped my mouth before I could control it.

Isha first glared at me but then smiled. oh fuck I'm in trouble.

"Hum logon ko Rasam thodi modify kardeni chahiyee right? I think Ansh ko bhi ye wali rasam karni chahiye ..." NO. nononoo... I'm even worse at cooking.

"Yeah right... jao ayaansh. both of you should do it." Maa said and I saw Isha smirk as she walked in the kitchen grabbing my hand, dragging me with her.

"bohot hasi aa rahi thi na patidev? ab khul kar hasiye... khaana banate hue." She said and settled on the counter expecting me to start cooking.

I should've protested but guess what? I actually started cooking.

"Dhang se banana..." She said glancing in the pan in which i was doing... ..something.

"Wow....You are such a controlling wife Isha. So toxic." I said and continued doing what i was doing. I glanced at her when she didn't reply only to see her eyes on me as if she was trying to figure something out.

"Why?" She asked me. I knew what was going on in her mind.

Doubt.

Questions.

Insecurity.

"What why?" I asked her despite knowing what her question will be.

"I know you Ayaansh. I know you better than anyone else." She said getting up from the counter.

That was true.

Ishani knew me like people knew the back of their hand.

She knew me more than i knew myself.

"Do anything that you want ansh... Just-Please don't pretend that you're in love with me." She said and i noticed that her voice broke in the end as she started opening random boxes.

Am I too torturous?

Was it that hard for her?

Where was this pain when she decided to hurt me? Where was it when she decided to hide things from me?

"Where was this pain when you decided to break my heart?" I said it. I finally said it.

"You are making it sound like I wanted to do it. I didn't." She said and a humorous chuckle left my mouth.

If she didn't want to do it then why did she do it.

She said she didn't have a choice but that's a lie.

If she just told me once, Just once that she needed help and i would've killed anyone for her.

"I loved you." Fuck, why would she say that? Why would she say something like that which is capable of making me feel guilty.

"Now you are acting as if i didn't love you." I said with a smile while she just stirred the halwa in the cooking pot in front of us.

"I never said that. I just wanted you to understand me for once. Just listen to my perspective and hear why i hid things from you." She said and asked the servants to serve the halwa when they go out.

"Fine then, You want us to have a chance right? Just answer one question truthfully." I asked as she turned around to face me.

"What were you so scared of?" I asked her the same question from 5 years ago.

I saw a lone tear roll down her cheek and when she spoke her voice was broken as if she was holding everything in "I don't have an answer to that."

"Then tell me when you find all those answers because I cannot love you again if everything we had was based on lies." That was all I could say before walking out of the kitchen.

Every word I said was true.

If she can't find the answers then I can't love her.

I have already spent years to get over the pain she caused me but this time it won't be easy for her.

[Ishani's pov...]

3 years ago...

Loneliness.

That was all I could feel in that moment.

Mom and Dad are gone.

They died last month.

They left me alone.

Pari is a mess and I am taking her to Delhi with me for a few months before she leaves for New York.

I knocked on Ayaansh's door in his home.

I needed some signatures related to the company coalition.

The last time we actually had a conversation without yelling was 2 years ago.

when we broke up.

shit, it hurts too much.

He opened the door and i saw his expressions come to neutral as he let me in.

"I need the coalition pa-" i began but he cut me off. again.

"I know." He didn't even look me in the eyes and was looking in a file.

My hands were shaking and it was very noticeable.

I was way too anxious around him. Way too anxious for my own good.

He handed me the papers but instead of walking out I stayed there. And he let me stay there.

"Ansh-" I began but couldn't complete my sentence as he cut me off.

"Please don't say it. Please." He knew what I was going to say. Something which I wasn't able to say for two years.

"Please ansh I need you."I said and tears were flowing freely out of my eyes as a sob escaped my throat.

I needed him in my life. I needed him to survive. I needed him.

"Even I needed you right? What did you do?" He asked and i bit my lip to stop the sob which was about to escape my mouth.

"Just one chance. That's all I ask you. Just one chance to let me explain myself." I said while looking down because I knew if I look at him for one more second, I'll break completely.

"How do you expect me to give you a chance if you don't have any answers. How do you think that you'll understand me if you can't understand yourself." I hated how true he was. But at the same time i just wanted to be there with him.

I just wanted him to be there even if he was just saying something which will hurt me.

"I love you." That was all I could say. I had no other words.

"But I don't." His words were piercing in my heart. It felt like thousands of knives were stabbing in it continuously.

"Then please let me love you...Please try to love me." I was begging him to love me again.

A princess never begs. That was the golden rule for everything.

But right now I was begging for love. I was begging the guy that i love to try and love me again.

"I can't. Not after what happened Isha... Please just get yourself out of this turmoil which you have created in your heart and mind in the past two years, It's killing you from inside. Loving me will only hurt you." His words were enough for me to lose every hope I had for us.

There was no good reason to think that we can ever exist again.

....

present

"Beta kha kyon nahi rahi ho?" I got out of the memory I was losing myself into when maa called me.

"Nahi woh bas aise hi....I just zoned out i guess." I said with the fakest smile possible and started eating the breakfast again.

Pari held my hand from under the table and whispered to me "Can we talk after breakfast?"

"You don't have to ask pari...I'm always free for you." I said and she nodded.

The breakfast went on smoothly while I was just zoned out most of the time.

The past moments from 3 years back keep on flashing in front of my eyes.

I still remember what I was actually feeling that day. I remember every single emotion

Empty.

Lonely.

Unloved.

Unwanted.

My thoughts were suffocating me but I took a deep breath calming my heart down as me and pari entered her room.

"Kya baat karni thi?" I asked her with a smile.

She looked very nervous when she spoke "Ishu main thode time ke liye delhi wali branch sambhalna chahti hoon."

"Haan toh isme itna nervous kyon ho rahi hai...Tell me kab jaana chahti hai? And kitne time ke liye?"I asked her, sitting down on the bed.

"Thode mahine maybe." she replied with a relieved smile.

"okay....now tell me the real reason." I asked her as she looked down, trying to hide her tears.

"it's nothing." she said but I knew she was lying..

"I'm your sister pari. You can't lie to me." That was all that i said as a tear dropped from her eye.

She leaned her head on my shoulder as i caressed her hair.

"I am not happy with my life ishu... There is nothing which makes me want to wake up in the morning." She said and my heart broke at her words.

My sister was dying inside, each day and I couldn't do anything about it.

"Why is being in love so tough?" That question of hers made me smile a little as if I was mocking myself.

"Radha-Krishna ki kahani pata hai?" I asked her knowing that she is the biggest krishna devotee.

"The greatest love story of all time..." She said and i could sense the smile in her voice.

"Krishna ji se kayi Raniyan pyaar karti thi...sabhi gopiyan...sabhi bhakt. Sab unse bohot pyaar karte the na?" I asked her and she got her head off my shoulder and nodded looking at me.

"Aur krishna ji kinse pyaar karte the?"I asked her and another beautiful smile graced her face.

"Radha Rani se..."She replied in a soft voice.

"Jab Radha Rani ki shaadi kisi aur se ho gayi....Yaani ki jab woh dono ek nahi ho paye tab wo dono bohot roye the..." I said and Pari frowned at my words "what do you mean ishu?"

"I mean ki..." i took a deep breath before continuing "pyaar ke liye toh bhagwaan bhi roye the....hum toh fir bhi insaan hain."

"But still Radha-Krishna ka naam saath mein liya jaata hai na?" She asked me and I smiled knowing that she got my point.

"That is exactly what i learnt in the past five years..."I said and she raised her eyebrows in confusion.

"I learnt that... if it's meant to be then it will find it's back to you no matter what."

----

now this chapter was intense.

Are you team Ayaansh or Team Ishani??

for reels and updates, follow me on Instagram: tithi._

love you lotssssss □□

13. Politics

[Ayaansh's Pov]

"Isha wake up!" I said for the thousandth time shaking Isha just slightly.

"No..." She said and turned around hugging my arm unconsciously.

"Uth jaa meri maa please!" I said tapping her cheeks a little.

"Kya hai yaar sone nahi de sakte..." She said and I looked at the clock again.

8:00 AM.

"Ishani wake up or else Dadisa will kill both of us." I said and she finally opened her eyes and looked at the clock.

She let out a sigh and groggily walked towards the bathroom.

Finally.

After about half an hour she walked out of the closet in her work clothes and rolled her eyes at me.

Is it my fault that she is a heavy sleeper who does not wake up even after 15 alarms?

A notification pinged on her phone while I was wearing my watch and she was brushing her hair.

"WHAT THE ACTUAL FUCK?" She literally yelled looking at her screen.

I really hope it's not a big mess.

"What happened? Is everything okay?" I asked and she showed me her phone.

It was an online news article.

"What the fuck." That was all I could say looking at the article.

It was a picture of Vihaan and Preksha.

In front of Ishani's office building.

They were Kissing!!!

....

"I want that picture off the internet in 15 minutes or else you'll be dead." Ishani said on her phone.

If glares could kill then my brother would've been 6 feet under the ground right now.

"Do you guys want to explain?" I said trying to be serious when all I wanted to do was to laugh out loud but if I did that then Isha will actually kill me.

"No." Preksha said and walked out of the room.

Wow.

"Do you want to explain something?" Isha asked Vihaan who just gulped and shook his head.

Vihaan was always scared of Isha for god knows what reason.

He said that he thinks that she will kill him with a glare.

"Whatever....is between me and preksha is a bit......complicated so-" Is he actually Vihaan because Vihaan never fumbles with his words.

"I don't care if you guys are dating or not but dare you to make her cry again and I will chop your head off and present it to the world." She would actually do that.

But what did she mean by Again?

"Yeah...okay bye." He said and literally ran out of the room.

Isha's glare shifted from Vihaan's retreating figure to me and she shook her head in a subtle disappointment before walking out.

"ab maine kya kiya?" I asked myself and took my car keys walking out of the room.

[Ishani's pov....]

Both of the Yaduvanshi Brothers are the same.

Idiots.

And now two monkeys are sitting in front of me munching on chips while not letting me work.

"Sun" Rashmi said and I took a deep breath calming myself down.

"Suna." I said still not looking up from the laptop.

"Aati kya khandala." Pari said and both of them giggled as if it was the funniest thing ever.

"Preksha is the presentation completed?" I asked her and she smiled.

"Yes and I mailed it to you too." Sometimes I forget that she is my sister.

"Rashmi don't you have work?" I said and her smile almost wiped off.

"Thanks for reminding me that I want to talk to both you and ayaansh tonight. Its important." She said and got up. If Rashmi stops smiling that means shit is actually wrong.

"Abhi nahi bata sakti?" I asked her with a frown and she shook her head walking out.

"What was that?" Pari asked me and before I could reply Vikram barged in the room.

"Shitij Rajwansh wants to meet you." I wanted to smash my head in a wall and jump off the building.

"Did he have an appointment?" I asked and Vikram shook his head negatively.

"Then tell him to get lost." I said with a smile and continued with my files.

"He's saying it's important and this can't wait that's why main yahaan aaya warna why would I disturb you for that moron?" He said and I sighed asking him to let Shitij come in.

"Good morning Rani Sa." He greeted and sat in front of me while his manager stood behind him.

"What do you want?" I asked him straightly getting to the point.

"Rude. But, I wanted to show this to you..." He said and gave a file to me.

My hands stilled as I saw the file.

Shitij's father, My uncle, was found dead today at 1:00 PM.

It was currently 2:00 PM.

This makes Shitij the new ruler of Mewad.

Nope. This can't be happening.

If he rules a city that means that the city will be destroyed.

"Sign on it." He almost ordered me which made me throw daggers at him with my eyes.

"Sure." I said with a smile signing the papers and Pari looked at me in shock.

"What is wrong with you Ishu?" She whispered to me and my smile grew.

I took out a pack of cigarettes from my drawer offering one to Shitij who happily took one.

I took out a lighter and lit the cigarette taking a puff and then took the papers back in my hand.

I flicked the lighter and burnt the papers throwing them on the floor.

"What the hell? You bitch." He yelled moving closer towards me but stopped at his place as I pointed my gun at him.

His manager's phone rang and his panicked face was a treat to watch as he answered the call.

"Sir, the building where you keep your documents and important files is on fire. It's almost completely burnt."

"You did that. You bitch! you did that, didn't you?" He asked and I shook my head frowning at him.

This is so fun.

"No I didn't. My husband did." I said with a smile and he said something to is manager who went out of the room.

"Politics is a dirty game Shitij." I said as his jaw clenched even more.

"But I can't believe you killed your own father for that." I said and he looked shocked.

"Stay out of my way." he said and rushed out of my office.

"You are one hell of a bitch." Pari said chuckling and i wrapped up my work texting a thank you to Ansh.

I got in the car with Pari and after about 30 minutes we reached home.

"I'm leaving next week after your reception." She said and I ruffled her hair with a smile.

As soon as we entered the house our smiles vanished.

Two people sitting in the living room laughing with Dadisa.

Jagrit and Neysa Chandramukhi.

Pari's Parents.

Assholes.

14. Heartfelt Conversations

Why the hell would Ishani call me and randomly ask me to burn a building down?

Well, I did it.

A text notification popped up on my phone screen while I was working on my laptop.

Isha: Come home right now. I can't deal with these shitheads alone.

Me: You hate a new person everyday. Mind telling me which shithead is it?

Isha: Jagrit and Neysa Chandramukhi.

Holy shit.

I need to go home.

Me: I'll be there in 10.

Preksha's parents are idiots.

They left their daughter and moved to a completely different city. They are emotionally abusive, manipulative bastards. They only care about money and fame. That's it.

Preksha is like a sister to me. I always wanted a younger sister but instead i got and idiotic, annoying brother who is apparently obsessed with Preksha.

Vihaan always followed Preksha around. I just didn't tell Isha because I didn't want my brother dead.

Upon reaching home I saw the whole family sitting in the dining room. Ishani signaled me to go change and when I came downstairs I was almost creeped out by the smiles the shitheads were giving me.

I silently sat on the dining table and their next words made everyone choke on their food.

"We were thinking that pari will turn 21 in a month so how about getting her married?"

What the fuck?

She was too young.

Me and Isha got married at a young age just for the sake of the throne otherwise none of us had a plan on getting married this early.

"Pari do you want to get married?" Ishani asked her and she immediately replied "No!"

"If she doesn't want to get married then she won't" I said and both of their faces show anger.

Preksha was too young to get married. She needs to build up her career and she was still not mature enough.

Me and Ishani, we had to grow up at a very young age due to unfortunate circumstances but we would not want that to happen with her too.

"Pari we are your parents and we know the best for you-" They have the fucking audacity to say stuff like this.

It happened. What I exactly thought would happen.

Preksha reached her breaking point.

"First of all, Stop calling me Pari. Only the people close to me can call me that, It's Preksha for you! Second of all, I would've let you make decisions for me if you didn't abandon me. The only people who can make decisions for me are dadi and ishu so don't you fucking dare. You are a pathetic, lame excuse of parents." She yelled and got up leaving the table.

Preksha was always the silent one. She never used to complain or let her emotions out so this break down was necessary for her.

Vihaan got up and went behind her. Isha was about to follow her but I held her hand stopping her.

"Vihaan will handle her, it's okay. She needs time." I whispered to her and she complied.

"I would advice you to leave our home as soon as possible or things might get ugly." Isha said and they immediately got up.

....

"How is she?" I asked Isha as soon as she entered the room.

"She is saying she's fine and that she'll be even better once she goes to Delhi." Isha said and came in the balcony, sitting on the chair in front of me.

"When is she leaving?" I asked putting my book away now looking at her who was massaging her scalp.

"Next week. After our Reception." She said and I got up moving behind her.

I put my hands in her hair and gently massaged her head. She sighed in relief leaning back against me.

"Ansh, I was thinking something today." She said looking up at me.

"What?" I asked her while massaging circles on her temples with my thumbs.

"Who was your first crush?" She asked me making me chuckle.

Was she really thinking about this today?

"It was a girl I met on a vacation when I was 6." I said truthfully and she turned her head towards me.

"You remember about her and you don't even remember my favorite dish!" She said looking at me looking absolutely adorable.

She's so cute.

"I have a sharp memory and your favorite dish is dal makhani." I said and she smiled.

Cute. Cute. Cute.

"Tell me about her. I want to know ki mere alawa kisne tumhara dil churaya?" She asked me looking the slightest bit of sad. I leaned down and kissed her cheek.

"I was 6, Isha. It was a silly liking." I said and she punched me in the stomach.

"Batao na..." She said and now her yes were droopy as she leaned her head back while I continued massaging her head.

"I was in Paris for a vacation when I was six. Me and maa-papa went to this shopping mall over there because maa needed to buy something. I was in the game zone with my caretaker while they shopped. I saw a girl, probably 5 years old, she was struggling with that game in which you pick up stuff toys with mechanical claws." I explained to her with a smile on my face remembering the hazy memory.

"I went to her and decided to help her out, and guess what? Your husband was so talented that I got the stuff toy in a single try. She even asked her caretaker to click our picture. I wanted to ask her name but she ran away with that polaroid picture." I told her and saw her smiling widely at me.

A smile which can brighten up anyone's day.

"Come with me, I'll show you something." She said and got inside our room and I followed, closing the balcony door.

She opened a drawer, taking out a journal. She frowned while looking through the pages and soon a smile made it's way on her face.

She took out a paper from the middle of the page and gave it to me.

It was a picture and when I turned the paper around to look at it, my heart stilled.

No. Fucking. Way.

It was a picture of me with that girl in the game zone.

That girl was my Isha.

Fuck.

"You're kidding me right?" I asked her still not being able to believe the coincidences.

That's why I wasn't able to recognize her because me and Isha met when I was 9.

"I was your first crush, ansh." She said closing the journal.

"First and Last." I said and looked at her.

Beautiful.

"Can I keep this picture?" I asked her and she nodded with a smile.

"You're sleepy Isha. Let's go to sleep." I said putting the picture in my wallet.

Suddenly her Alarm rang and she smiled switching it off. She grabbed my bicep and pulled me towards her.

Her lips connected with mine and it felt like heaven. I stilled for a second when I realized that she kissed me.

Her lips slowly moved over mine and molded as if they were meant to be kissed by me.

It was true. Her lips were meant to be kissed by me.

My hands went on her waist pulling her closer to me, her body flushed against mine.

After a few seconds she pulled back and I connected her forehead with mine as her breathing evened.

Her hand slowly caressed my jaw and my eyes fluttered close.

How can this woman be so loving yet so dangerous? And her next words made me smile.

"Happy Birthday Ansh."

15. I'm sorry

‑‑

(Ayaansh's POV...)

Last week after my birthday was a complete mess. It just comprised three things:

WorkWorkWork

I had to go to the office early and come back late, then Isha yells at me for being late all the time but then says she doesn't care.

Our reception is tomorrow and Rashmi called both of us immediately for something.... important.

"Mind telling me why you called me back home in the middle of a meeting?" I asked, earning a scoff from the angry woman sitting beside me.

"At least you came home." Isha said with a huff.

"I come home every day. It's not my fault that you fall asleep as soon as you hit the bed and don't wake up till I threaten you by calling Dadisa!" I said and she dramatically gasped as if I said something wrong.

"You asshol-" She began to curse me but fortunately Rashmi stopped her before my ears start to bleed.

"Tum dono pati-patni baad mein jhagda kar lena. Now, listen to me." She said moving across the table and standing in front of us.

"I found out something and it might be triggering for both of you." She said with a hint of uncertainty in her voice.

And her next words made me stiffen.

"You see, this whole threat you got from that Omkar Srivastava guy and the threats which Ishani got 5 years ago regarding her parents were interconnected."

Why? Why why why why?

Why does everything have to come back to the same spot?

Why does everything have to hurt so much even after so many years?

"Um- why- I mean how?"Isha asked her and even if I was not looking at her, I knew she was fiddling with her fingers at the moment.

And I knew what she was thinking.

"We investigated everything and I am pretty sure that the people who killed your grandparents and your sister are the ones who trapped those girls for so many months." Okay, that's enough. Too much for today.

"Someone wants to finish the whole Royal family." Rashmi said and I got up from my chair making my way to my bedroom.

Everything will be okay.

Things don't repeat right?

History doesn't repeat itself.

Atleast I hope it doesn't.

I've already had enough.

I don't think I can handle anything more.

At the age of 18 my grandparents died, my sister, her name was Aria, she died.

My love betrayed me.

At the age of 20 my father lost all of his trust on me.

I lost every hope that I might be able to fix everything with my Isha.

I lost everything and now you can only describe me as a person who's dead from inside.

My hand instinctively went towards the photo frame on my bedside table.

Our room had a lot of pictures.

Our wedding photo and our engagement picture. A few more of our pictures, A photo of Isha and Preksha, A photo of me and Vihaan. A picture of me with my mother. Not with my father though, he doesn't even talk to me if it's not about work.

Aria's picture.

"I'm sorry Aria. I'm so damn sorry that I was not a good brother."

A traitor tear left my eye but I wiped it off.

No more tears.

I shed enough of them.

I heard the door opening but I didn't look back.

A hand draped on my shoulder and I knew it was her. I could recognise her at any given time.

"I really miss all of them." It was a mere whisper on my lips but I really needed to say it.

"I miss them too" She said but I was not sure if she meant it.

Did she mean it?

I moved back and took out my jacket from the closet.

I need to take fresh air.

I needed to breath.

"Ayaansh, I'm sorry." She said and her voice broke in the end.

Ayaansh.Ayaansh.Ayaansh.

A failure Ayaansh.A disappointment Ayaansh.

A bad son.A bad brother.A bad husband.

"It doesn't matter anymore." That's all I said before closing the door.

And that was the first night I didn't go back home.

I couldn't.I just couldn't.

(Ishani's POV...)

He didn't come back home last night.

I waited but he didn't.

And eventually I dozed off to sleep with just one thought in my mind...

Ayaansh.

My love.

The person who doesn't even trust me anymore.

But it's okay.

I can handle it. Right?

My eyes fluttered open with a faint noise in the dressing room.

I was on the bed.

I slept on the sofa while waiting for him.

Okay, he was back.

He came out of the dressing room and took a glance at me before averting his gaze back at the mirror, running a hand through his hair.

"When did you come back?" I asked before getting off the bed.

"An hour ago." How can he answer so casually?

"Where were you last night?" I asked as my curiosity seeped in.

"Bike ride." What the actual hell?

"The whole night? You must be exhausted!" I said but he just tied his watch around his wrist.

"I'm not." Why is he so distant all of a sudden?

We were at too much distance for five years and just when I thought that everything was going amazing he just vanishes for the whole night.

Was it because of yesterday?

If yes then why is he not answering me?

I don't blame him though.

His grandparents were gone because of me.

Aria was gone because of me.

But don't I get a chance to explain myself?

"Stop." He said making me come out of my thoughts.

"Kya?" I asked and he sighed before leaning in and placing the softest kiss on my cheek.

So we are okay? Are we?

"I can literally feel you overthinking. Stop it." He said caressed my hair and placed another kiss on my forehead.

And then he did the most unexpected thing.

He hugged me.

"Just promise me one thing, Isha." He said and nodded, placing my head on his chest.

"Never, and I mean it, never repeat the same mistake." He said making me still at my place.

"Just because I am trying to forget everything doesn't mean that it's easy to heal." He said and I tried my best not to cry.

Not at the hurt which I was feeling but at the pain he had held for so long.

The pain that I gave him.

The pain which destroyed both of us from within.

And the worst part is that I don't even know how to fix everything.